A CRONGTON CHRISTMAS PARTY

Also by Alex Wheatle:

Crongton series:
Liccle Bit
Crongton Knights
Straight Outta Crongton
In The Ends

Home Girl

The Girl With the Red Boots

ALEX WHEATLE

A CRONGTON CHRISTMAS PARTY

HODDER CHILDREN'S BOOKS

First published in Great Britain in 2025 by Hodder & Stoughton Limited

1 3 5 7 9 10 8 6 4 2

Text copyright © Alex Wheatle, 2025
Cover illustration copyright © Berat Pekmezci, 2025

The moral right of the author has been asserted.

*All characters and events in this publication, other than those clearly
in the public domain, are fictitious and any resemblance to
real persons, living or dead, is purely coincidental.*

All rights reserved.
No part of this publication may be reproduced, stored in a retrieval system,
or transmitted, in any form or by any means, without the prior permission
in writing of the publisher, nor be otherwise circulated in any form of binding
or cover other than that in which it is published and without a similar condition
including this condition being imposed on the subsequent purchaser.

A CIP catalogue record for this book
is available from the British Library.

ISBN 978 1 444 96218 5

Typeset in in 11/16pt Palatino LT Std by Six Red Marbles UK, Thetford, Norfolk
Printed and bound in Great Britain by Clays Ltd, Elcograf S.p.A.

The paper and board used in this book
are made from wood from responsible sources.

Hodder Children's Books
An imprint of
Hachette Children's Group
Part of Hodder & Stoughton Limited
Carmelite House
50 Victoria Embankment
London EC4Y 0DZ

The authorised representative in the EEA is Hachette Ireland,
8 Castlecourt Centre, Dublin 15, D15 XTP3, Ireland (email: info@hbgi.ie)

An Hachette UK Company
www.hachette.co.uk

www.hachettechildrens.co.uk

To all those who have felt lonely during any holiday or festival. This one's for you.

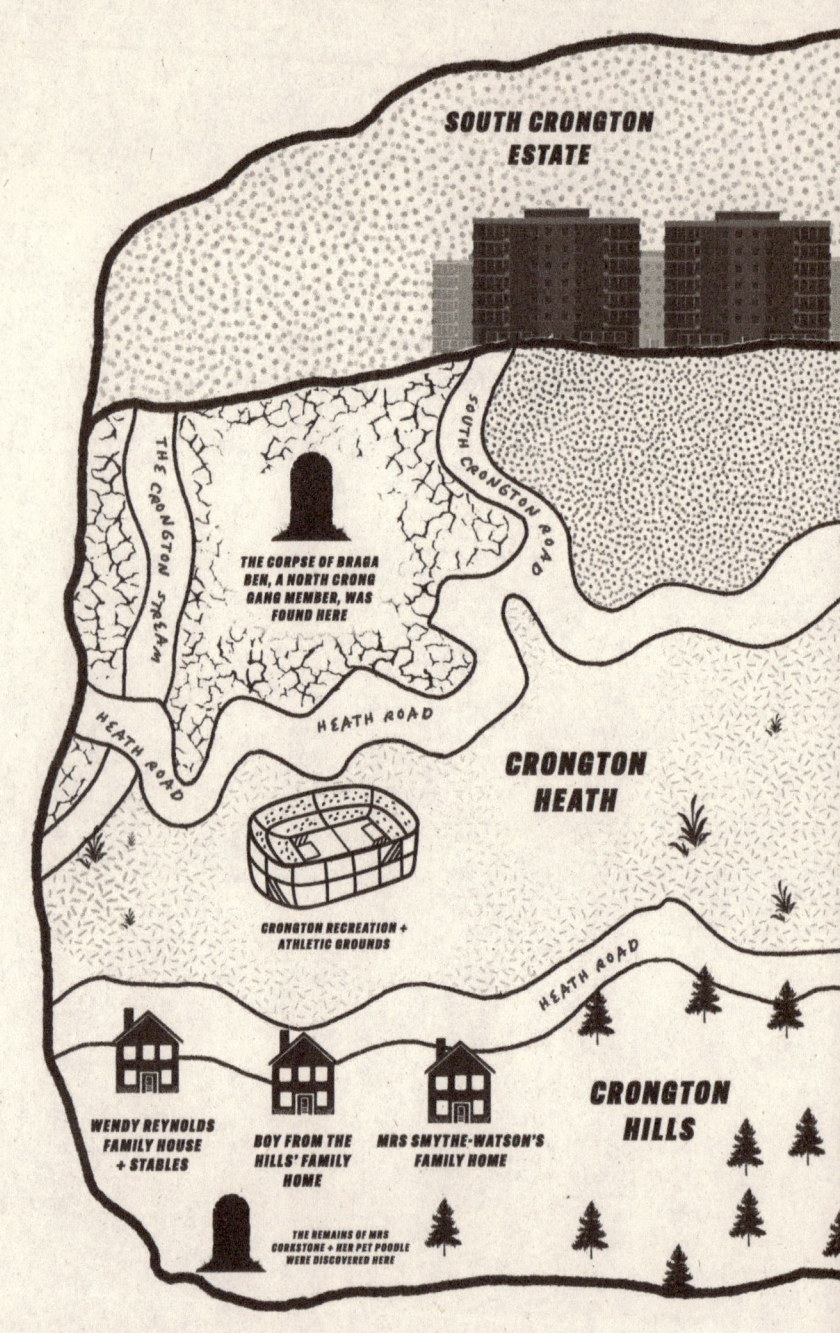

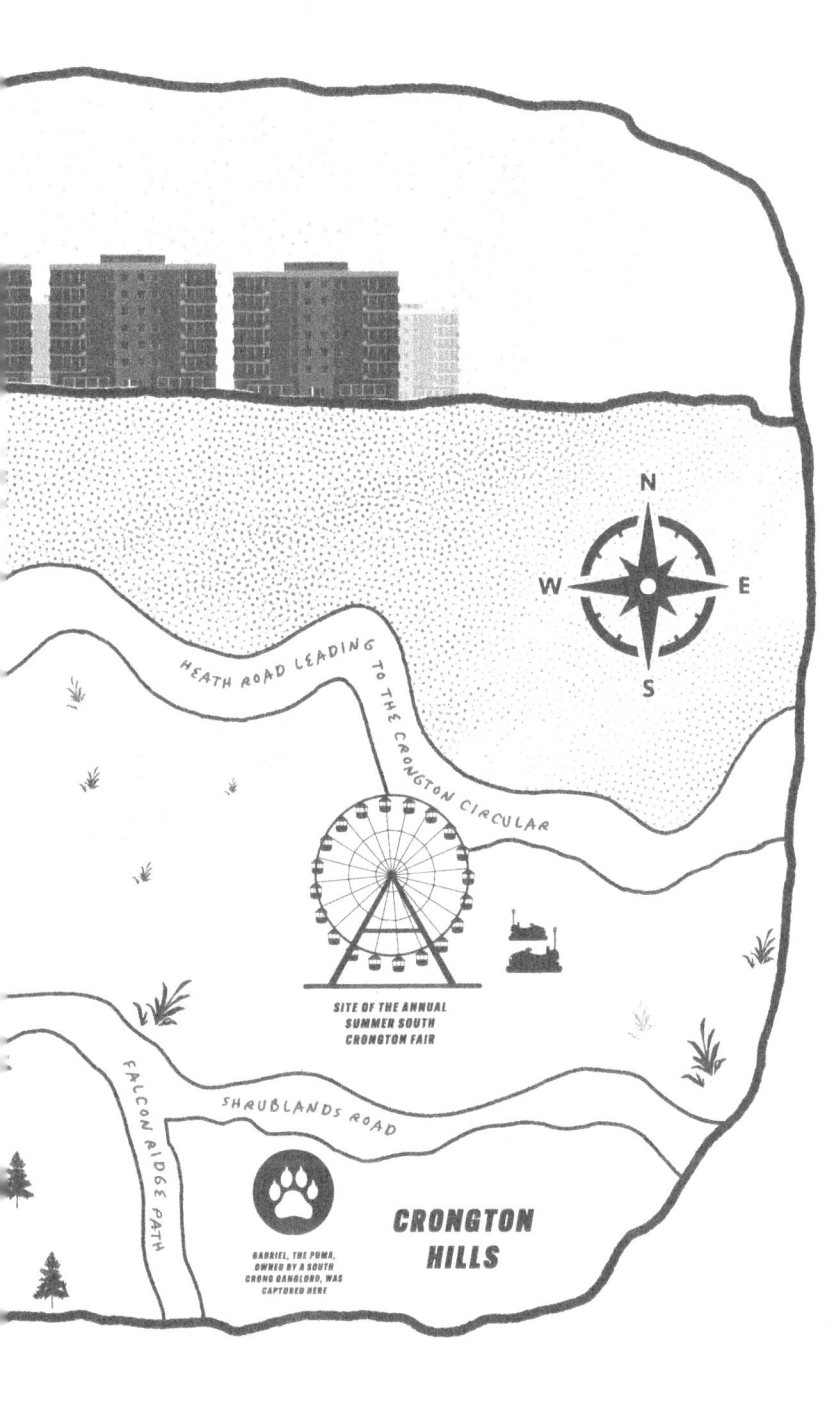

My name is Gordon Colin Scott. Some broccoli brains at school say I only look twelve, but I'm fourteen years old. I turn fifteen next March. I prefer folks to call me Colin cos it doesn't sound as posh as Gordon. At school, because of my wild hair, I was christened 'Boy from the Hills'. It kinda stuck. I don't mind it too much. I'd rather have a nickname than folks not even noticing me.

I live by Crongton Heath in a six-bedroom mansion with a gravel driveway and a circular front lawn. I attend South Crongton High School. I do my best to keep my address on the low profile, otherwise South Crong estate kids would take the living piss out of me.

Already I've been called 'Glory Tory Boy', 'Lord of the Squires' and 'Billionaire Kid'.

My dad is a top-rated barrister and my mum's a

psychiatrist. I don't know how much they're worth, but my dad keeps an Aston Martin DB5 that he never drives in the garage. His friends love to wheel it out and sit in it. I laugh to myself when they pretend to be James Bond. I'm not even allowed to touch the damn thing. My mum books last-minute-dot-com holidays to places like Tibet and Peru. She likes hiking up hills and going camping.

My parents are hardly home these days. They're always going on this campaign or that march. When I complain about it, they say, 'What's the problem? Do you realise how lucky you are? You have everything you want.'

At school, my best friends are McKay, Jonah, Liccle Bit, Venetia, Saira and Juniper. I've been through dramas with all of them. Last time, I barely escaped with my young life. We had to hot-bike it away from Fireclaw Heath, trying to get away from G-Gore's Notre Dame crew.

Oh, my daisies, that was a close one.

It scared the ribs out of me, but it was much more exciting than watching Dad and Mum entertain guests at their boring dinner parties. They expect me to play the perfect son, but sometimes I'm tempted to place bull-crap on their well-expensive dinner seats.

Nearby lives Wendy Reynolds. Her parents are horsey folk. She spends more time on a nag than she does walking. She comes around now and again to watch films on my big screen in the basement. She's the only friend I have around these rich ends. I can't lie, I have a thing for her. I haven't told her yet. Probably never will. Other local kids think I'm weird.

Things have calmed down between the gangs of North and South Crong. The king G of South Crong, Manjaro, is now staring at a long sentence, and we haven't heard much about Major Worries in North Crong. The feds patrol the streets of South Crong much more frequently these days.

Nobody has been deleted for months. There was a shanking in Crong Park in November, but it wasn't gang related. It was over a girl.

As Christmas approaches, me and my friends have started to relax and live the good life. We've been making plans for the holidays. Venetia has made me promise that I'll do something with my hair for her dad's Christmas church service. I said to her that I'll think about it. She punched me in the arm. 'You better! You're not gonna embarrass me!'

'Twas the week before Christmas. I never imagined that my life was about to get cradazily dramatic again. And what's more, the headlights would be on my ass instead of one of my friends.

1

Bossi the Boerboel

Thursday.

School had finished for the day. Only one more day to go before we broke up. My friends and I linked up just outside the school gates. Liccle Bit had a blob of blue paint on his cheek. I sniffed something tasty coming from McKay's bag. Banana cake? Juniper wore different brand trainers on each foot.

'Is everyone on it then?' asked Liccle Bit. 'Cinema on Saturday?'

'I don't wanna see no boring Christmas romcom movie,' moaned Jonah. 'Why can't we see something with a bit more action?'

'Because the world is about more than Avengers, Spider-Men and Black Panthers,' said Venetia. 'For once in our lives, can't we watch an everyday romcom? Or even a Christmas movie.'

'Jonah, you might learn something,' joked McKay.

'Boy from the Hills,' called Saira. 'What about you? What do you wanna watch?'

'Er . . . I'm easy either way,' I said. 'If pushed, I nudge towards something with a dose of action.'

'Yes!' said Jonah.

'Juniper?' asked Liccle Bit. 'What say you?'

Juniper twirled her green and purple hair around her fingers. She offered a mischievous smile. 'There's this horror film,' she said. *'It Came Out of the River.* A lot of people die cos this thing pollutes whatever it touches. Faces fall off and all that. Politicians' fingers and hands just drop off. It sounds so cool.'

'I'm not gonna watch a horror movie over Christmas,' said Venetia.

'Venetia, you're not being diverse enough,' argued Juniper. 'These days horror movies don't get any love. It's not like there's a guy in it who deletes kids with a long blade at some cabin by a lake.'

'Can we have a vote on this?' asked Liccle Bit. 'Hands up for the romcom.'

Venetia and Liccle Bit raised their hands. After a bit of thought, McKay and Saira put up their hands too.

'Who wants to go for that action movie,' asked Liccle Bit. 'What's it called again?'

'Escape from Littleville Mall,' replied Jonah. 'It's about how this heroic guy who works in an Apple store helps to kill this other guy who goes on a shooting rampage. He's just armed with one of those cardboard cutter things.'

Only Jonah and I raised our hands for that one.

'So only me wants to see *It Came Out of the River*?' asked Juniper. 'You don't know the ending of that one and who's gonna survive. In your romcom, the boy gets the girl or the girl gets the boy. End of.'

'Or girl might get girl and boy might get boy,' said Saira.

'OK,' said Liccle Bit. 'So romcom it is then. Let's meet Saturday on Crong Broadway. Evening showing is seven-fifteen.'

'I'm gonna smuggle in my snacks,' said McKay. 'Not paying those extortion rates for popcorn or a dog roll. Scandalous!'

McKay shared out slices of banana cake before we said our goodbyes. It was good.

I was the only one from my school who lived on the southside of the Heath. I took the shortcut through the long grass where dog folk walked their Saint Bernard mutts and Afghan Hounds, and young couples made out in the summer.

Reaching home twenty minutes later, I found Mum and Dad loading the green Range Rover with cabin cases and crates of tinned food. The Christmas lights on the naked cherry trees lit up the front lawn.

Dad was in his tear-up jeans and raggedy pullover. Mum wore her rubber boots, corduroy trousers and body warmer.

'Where're you going?' I asked.

'The Highlands,' replied Dad. 'A little north of Aberdeen. There's this company that's polluting the local river for fun and we're—'

A Crongton Christmas Party

'Going to support a campaign,' I finished the sentence. 'Are you going to save the little fishes and liberate little Loch Ness monsters?'

'No need to be sarcastic, Colin,' Mum said. 'It's important. You must make a stand on these things. These big companies can't be allowed to get away with it. If there's enough of us, the media will get hold of it.'

'And run the story,' added Dad.

'It's only a week till Christmas,' I said. 'When are you back?'

Mum and Dad swapped a glance. I guessed they wanted each other to answer my question.

'Christmas Eve,' Mum finally replied. 'We've invited friends up there on various days. It'll be rude to leave early.'

'That's . . . six days,' I said. 'What am I supposed to do? Step to Lapland and ask Santa if I can volunteer this year?'

'Maria has agreed to stay over until we get back,' said Dad. 'We're giving her a nice Christmas bonus.'

'We've also left fifty pounds with Maria in case you want a couple of friends over one evening,' said Dad. 'You can buy snacks or a takeaway and play pool or something. Don't they enjoy that?'

'Er, yes, they do,' I said. 'But that's just the one evening.'

'Oh, and Mrs Utili wants to see you,' said Mum. 'She asked me to give her a call as soon as you came home from school.'

'No!' I protested. 'I'm not doing it!'

'Doing what?' Dad asked.

'Looking after her dog. Definitely not. It's Christmas time. I'm going to the movies with my friends on Saturday, and then I'm going to church on Sunday morning to watch my friend do a solo.'

'Church?' Mum repeated. She looked baffled. 'You never go to church.'

'It could be something else other than dog-sitting,' said Dad. 'She might have a job for you in her back garden or in her big greenhouse. I thought you enjoy that kind of thing? You know, landscaping and all that.'

'No, she's gonna ask me to look after that monster of a dog of hers while she goes shopping in Paris or something. Not doing it! And it's the wrong time of year for landscaping.'

'She might pay.' Mum smiled.

'And her dog, Bossi, is so tame,' added Dad. 'He's so playful. Just remember to feed him on time.'

'He's lovely,' said Mum. 'And she hasn't got anyone else. She can't leave him alone. It's been tough for her since her husband died.'

'Her husband was thirty-seven years older than her,' I said. 'He smoked thirty a day and was ripe for a heart attack. What did she expect?'

Mum shook her head. 'That's unkind, Colin.'

'She did make you soup the last time you had flu,' Dad reminded me. 'She checked in every day with you while you were sick.'

'Yeah, she did.' I nodded. 'Cos you two were too busy!'

Dad shook his head.

Two seconds of silence.

Mum broke it. 'One good turn deserves another,' she said.

'But that dog's a monster! I'm not even sure if it's a dog. It's something between Godzilla and a Tasmanian devil.'

My parents laughed.

'You'll be fine,' said Mum. 'What more could you want? You'll have the house to yourself, you can have a couple of friends over, and you can watch what you want on the big screen in the games room. We've just downloaded new films on to the hard drive. Most kids would—'

'Love that opportunity,' I finished the sentence. 'Blah de blah blah. I've seen this movie.'

Mum took out her phone and called Mrs Utili.

'Yes,' she said. 'Merry Christmas to you too! Of course Colin will look after Bossi. He's looking forward to it . . . Yes, we know Bossi's as gentle as a cuddly toy. Of course, he won't feed him rubbish . . . only what you ask for. Bring him straight around. I'm sure Colin would like the company.'

My Christmas is dead. Bossi will be taking me for walks. He might eat me. Maybe I'll slap a saddle on him and join Wendy Reynolds when she rides out her horses. Then again, I should take him to school. No bullies will trouble me when they see Bossi.

Dad placed the last crate into the boot and stepped up to me. 'We're trying to raise an independent-thinking young man,' he said. 'One who stands on his own feet and appreciates his privilege.'

'All I ever do is appreciate my privilege,' I snapped. 'It should've been my middle name.'

'Yes.' Mum nodded. 'You'll soon be a man. I don't want you to be like the other spoilt kids around here.'

'No chance there,' I replied.

Mum hugged and kissed me on the cheek. 'Be good. Maria has finished the decorations. It's beginning to look a lot like Christmas.'

'If you do have one or two friends over,' Dad said. '*Don't* let them inside the garage. Is that clear? I've just had the DB5 waxed.'

'It's clear, Dad. You don't have to remind me.'

'There aren't too many original Aston Martin DB5s left in the UK,' Dad said.

'So you keep saying,' I replied. 'You have a nice time with slugs and ugly things that live at the bottom of the river. You obviously love to spend more time—'

'Colin!' Mum told me off. 'That's enough.'

Dad started the car and pulled away. He left gravel dust in his wake. A deep part of me wanted them to stay, but my brain screamed at me to enjoy my freedom.

What freedom? Bossi's gonna take up all my free time.

I went inside and headed for the kitchen. We had three Christmas trees: one by the staircase, another in the lounge and a smaller one in the dining area. They were all real. Mum had chopped them down herself. Not too much caring for the environment there.

Maria hadn't cooked anything.

'Maria! Maria!'

No response.

I headed to the basement. There she was, watching an episode of the *Power Universe* on the big screen. Tommy had just killed another of his enemies.

'Maria, what's for dinner?'

She was holding a gold star and had a bit of glitter in her black hair.

'No dinner today,' she said, staring at the screen. 'Takeaway. What do you want?'

'Er . . . I dunno. What do you want?'

Before she could answer, the doorbell rang.

'I'll get it,' I said.

I opened the front door. Mrs Utili wore knee-length black boots, brown leather trousers and something white and furry that a polar bear might have been missing. Tiger-striped earmuffs covered her ears. Her long black hair was tied into a ponytail.

'Merry Christmas!' she greeted in her Italian accent. 'Buon Natale!'

'Merry Christmas,' I replied.

Bossi looked a bit sleepy beside her. He was sitting down but his head almost reached the shoulder of his owner. He had a brown coat, but his nose, mouth and cheeks were black. His paws were about the same size as a rhino's foot.

I'm not scooping up anything that he craps. It must be enormous.

Mrs Utili bent down, grabbed Bossi by the neck and kissed him on the cheek. This monster tongue came out of Bossi's mouth and slobbered Mrs Utili's face. She seemed to enjoy it.

If he does that to me, I'll cut his tongue off!

'Your parents said it's OK for you to look after my sweet Bossi until Boxing Day,' she said.

'Boxing Day!' I repeated. 'You're going away for a week?'

'Sì,' Mrs Utili replied. 'I'm off to Salzburg. That city knows how to celebrate Christmas with all the Mozart music and festivals.'

'Boxing Day!' I said again.

'Sì, and it's been snowing there recently. It'll look very pretty. I'll be dancing to the music. Bella!'

'Can't you take Bossi with you?' I asked.

Mrs Utili angled her head and thought about it. 'Bossi doesn't like travelling too much. It upsets him. He would miss running about the Heath and the woods around here.'

'I haven't got any dog food,' I said. 'Can't feed him.'

'Oh, nessun problema,' replied Mrs Utili. 'Earlier I dropped off Bossi's food to Maria – rabbit and duck meat. It's in your fridge. Make sure you bring it to the boil and let it simmer for an hour or so. Serve it with a bit of gravy.'

'I have to cook?'

'Sì.' Mrs Utili nodded. 'Your parents said you'll be OK with that.'

'I'm not a good cook. In fact, I'm a bad, bad cook. I have issues boiling an egg.'

Mrs Utili smiled. Bossi licked his cheeks and stood up on his hind legs. I'm sure he could pull Santa's sleigh on his own.

Maybe he could hunt for his own food. There's plenty of foxes and rabbits around here.

'As it's Christmas, I will pay you,' she said.

She handed over an envelope. It was sealed. By the feel of it there were more than four notes in it.

They'd better not be fivers!

'Take him for walks first thing in the morning and at about six at night,' Mrs Utili instructed. She handed me a roll of green toilet bags and a scoop shovel. 'If you don't . . . well, you know what might happen.'

'Yeah, I know,' I replied.

The mischievous side of me was tempted to lock him up in my parents' bedroom. Bossi could do his business there.

Mrs Utili stooped down to kiss Bossi one last time. Bossi stuck his mega-tongue into her left ear.

Eeeeewwww!

'Arrivederci,' she said. 'Buon Natale!'

She handed over Bossi, turned and left. Bossi simpered and pulled a bit on his lead. I led him into the house and closed the double doors.

The lead was as thick as a rope.

I took him downstairs.

Maria paused her show. 'I know what you're going to ask,' she said. 'Here's the deal. I'll cook his rabbit and duck meat and you take him for walks.'

'That's good with me.' I nodded.

'For a price!' Maria added. 'That thing should really be showjumping.'

I opened my envelope. I counted one hundred and forty pounds.

Wow!

'Fifty pounds!' Maria demanded.

'Forty,' I replied.

'Fifty!'

'Forty-five,' I negotiated.

'Fifty!' Maria insisted. 'You'll be going to school tomorrow, the cinema on Saturday *and* you'll be going to your friend's church service on Sunday morning. Fifty!'

'Keep the fifty Mum and Dad gave you for when my friends come over,' I said. 'I'll keep the one hundred and forty.'

'Hmmmm.'

'Is that a "yes"?' I asked.

'Depends how well that thing behaves,' Maria replied. 'I reserve the right to change my mind.'

For a moment, I loosened my grip on Bossi's lead, and he headed for underneath the pool table. He made himself snug and closed his eyes. Ten minutes later he was asleep.

This might be easier than I thought. A sleepy hound is a good hound.

An hour or so later, Maria had boiled Bossi's duck meat and placed it in a large soup bowl. He sunk it in about three minutes. Our nearest neighbours were fifty metres away but I'm sure they heard Bossi licking his lips.

For my own dinner, Maria ordered Chinese: I had chow mein with spring rolls. Meanwhile, Bossi went back under the pool table and got his nap on.

I had to wake him up for his evening stroll at 6 p.m. I tried to walk him through the Heath, but he wasn't having it. He dragged me to the woods. He sniffed, farted, scared the living kidneys out of other hounds and did his business. At least in the woods I didn't have to scoop anything. And, my God, Bossi could crap a heavy load.

By the time I returned home, my arms felt like I had pulled in a cruise ship. Maria had placed an old blanket under the pool table. After nosing around the empty Chinese food cartons in the kitchen, Bossi crashed out.

Yes!

I played some pool before I went to bed. My head hit my pillow as I wondered what my friends would think about Bossi. If Maria changed her mind, I wouldn't make the cinema and Venetia's solo at church.

Could I take him with me? Tie him up outside the church? No, bad idea. He'll scare away the congregation.

2

Party Time

Friday morning. Six days before Christmas.

First lesson of the day was biology. All my friends had opted out of it, but from the very start, I loved to learn how living things work and grow. Splitting animals apart was gross at first, but after a while, I found it fascinating.

Now we were studying evolution and how the human body had changed over thousands of years.

At break, I was the first out of the door – I had to find my crew. I didn't want to tell them my breaking news about having to look after Bossi in a group text.

Blam!

I ran into the back of Vincent Chapman.

Oh no!

He dropped to one knee, almost falling over.

'Sor-sorry,' I managed.

Vincent looked at me like I had pissed in his favourite soup. He always rolled up the sleeves of his school blazer to show off his thick forearms. He was the second-best shot-putter in the school. He was only fifteen. 'I'll have to dry-clean my blazer now!' he said. 'It's polluted. You know how much that costs these days? No, you wouldn't! Cost of living crisis doesn't touch your squire boy behind.'

'Yeah.' His friend Donald Thompson nodded. 'Well expensive. Especially after you polluted it.'

They both blocked my way. I glanced behind me to see if there were any teachers about. There weren't. Other students kept a safe distance from us.

Vincent's blue eyes narrowed. His blonde hair was nearly as long as mine. 'That'll be a brown note, Mr Squire Boy.'

'You know I don't carry cash,' I replied. 'Especially ten-pound notes.'

'That's not our problem,' said Donald Thompson. He stepped towards me and reached out his hand. His lopsided Afro still didn't look right, but I'd never tell him. 'Pay your tax by the end of the day, otherwise there'll be interest.'

'Yeah,' Vincent chuckled. 'Fifty per cent.'

Donald clenched his fist. 'Otherwise, you know what's coming,' he added.

I glanced over my shoulder again. Mr Soares, my biology teacher, had just come out of his classroom.

'You can fling that tax and fifty per cent where the devil sleeps!' I said to Vincent. 'See ya later, gangster fakers!'

Party Time

I hot-footed it past Mr Soares along the corridor and into the playground. I frantically searched for my friends.

Relief.

There they were by the table tennis tables. Jonah was playing against Liccle Bit. McKay, Saira and Venetia watched.

I panted for a few breaths before I could say anything.

'I'm in a situation,' I said eventually.

Liccle Bit caught the ping-pong ball. Everyone looked at me.

'What kinda situation?' asked Jonah.

'I have to babysit a dog,' I revealed. 'And it's not a little poodle.'

Venetia stepped towards me, hands on hips. She had red, white and black coloured braids in her hair – the Trinidad colours. 'Does this mean you're not coming to my solo ting? Look how much notice I gave you! I told you weeks ago. You don't wanna go cos you don't wanna do something with your hair.'

'No, no. Maria should be able to look after him,' I said. 'My parents set it up. I didn't know a damn diddly till I got home from school yesterday. That's when they hit me with it. It's a neighbour's dog.'

'Did it eat your homework too?' asked McKay.

'Hate dogs,' said Saira. 'Can't believe you have to spend Christmas with one of them.'

'I'm getting paid,' I admitted. 'Getting paid neatly.'

'You are?' said Jonah, stepping towards me. His eyes lit up. 'You need any help?'

'Er . . .' I said.

'How much are you getting paid?' McKay asked.

'Er . . . one hundred and forty.'

'One hundred and forty!' Jonah repeated. 'For looking after a hound?'

'It's not your normal hound,' I replied.

'Care folk get less than that for looking after grey people,' Jonah went on. 'I'd babysit a man-eating tiger for that kinda money.'

'I'll . . . I'll be on my lonesome,' I said. 'My parents have gone away till Christmas Eve. To make up for it, they've said you can all come around to my place over the holidays to hang out. I've got funds for takeaways. We can shoot some pool and watch a few films. What do you say?'

McKay nodded. Something brewed inside his head. He then broke out into a wide smile. 'You know what I'm thinking?' he said.

'What's for school dinner today and how you're gonna complain about it?' laughed Liccle Bit.

'A Christmas cake?' wondered Saira.

'That new blueberry cheesecake that is on discount at the Cheesecake Lounge?' asked Venetia.

'No.' McKay shook his head. 'I'm thinking . . . party!'

'You're . . . you're not serious?' I replied.

'I'm double serious,' replied McKay. 'From the moment I planted my toes in your palace, I thought, great place for a party.'

Party Time

'My parents said I could have one or two friends over,' I said. 'That's all.'

'They left you in Christmas week,' Jonah said. 'That's cold.'

'Brutal,' added Liccle Bit.

'Neglect!' McKay shouted.

'They're always going away and leaving you on your lonesome,' said Saira. 'It's not right. Do they care more about their campaigns than you?'

'And you can't choose just two of us to enter your gates,' Jonah said.

'Yeah.' McKay nodded. 'We Crongton Knights are a package. It's the perfect situation for a party.'

'And it's gotta be a fancy-dress party,' said Juniper.

Where did Juniper come from? Jonah has a point about the package thing. I can't invite two to my gates and leave the others out.

'Doesn't a party mean music, food and stuff?' I asked.

'DJ Teaspoon!' jumped in Venetia. 'He's got a laptop and beats. Sometimes, he helps us out with music for our dance lessons. We can ask him.'

'DJ Teaspoon?'

'He's in our year,' said Liccle Bit. 'Tall, mixed-race brother. He's always wearing headphones. Loves his coffee.'

'How comes I've never heard of him?' I said.

'He's only had one proper gig,' replied Saira. 'At the reopening of the youth club. He played a set, and it went down well. He got South Crongton folk fizzing and bubbling.'

'And how much is he gonna cost?' I wanted to know.

'He'll do it for free,' said Venetia. 'He's trying to make a name for himself.'

'And I can do the food,' offered McKay. 'I'm gonna try out my new spicy chicken rolls and I'll bake my mince pies. We'll get some patties in too. You've got a whop-a-duper budget. One hundred and forty pounds. That'll cover all the ingredients and soft drinks we need. And there's enough space in your oven to cook a buffalo.'

'And Brontosaurus ribs,' added Juniper.

'I'll have to ask Maria,' I said.

'She works for your family,' said Jonah. 'Works for *you*. We've had untold near-death experiences this year with G-Gore and other dramas. Can't we finish the year with a party?'

'A fancy-dress party,' added Juniper. 'Like it's 2199.'

I thought about it.

'Will you guys help me clean up afterwards?'

'Of course,' replied Saira. 'As if we wouldn't.'

'And we can't let Vincent Chapman and Donald Thompson know,' I said. 'I've already got on their demon side by crashing into them just a minute ago. I don't want them two coming around to my gates and terrorising everyone.'

'News about your party is not gonna leak from me,' promised Venetia.

'Nor me,' said Saira. She made a zipping motion over her mouth.

'Yes!' said McKay. 'When are you gonna give me the funds to do the shopping?'

'We'll go before the cinema, so we're not eating into Venetia's singing thing on Sunday,' I replied.

'Thing!' Venetia repeated. 'Thing! I'll be singing a solo carol. *God Rest Ye Merry, Gentlemen.*'

'Aren't there any carols about merry women?' asked Saira.

No one could provide an answer.

'When the holidays are done,' I said, 'someone might rap about a kid being swallowed by a great hound.'

'Stop griping,' Jonah said. 'You're getting paid neatly.'

'Before you get munched,' Venetia cut in, 'fix up your hair and step to the church to hear my solo.'

'Catch up when school is done?' asked McKay.

'Yeah,' I replied. 'But I can't hang for too long. Got to take Bossi for his evening trod.'

'See you at the cinema as well,' Venetia said. 'You always say you never get invited to stuff. Well, you are now.'

I nodded. 'I'll remind Maria to look after Bossi when I get home.'

'And don't forget to do something with your hair!'

3

Timber!

Maths was my last lesson of the day. It kinda bored me but I needed to learn how to work out angles and curves if I was ever gonna design folks' gardens. I thought about the party.

Yeah, it'll be cool. My parents have gone way up north to have their kinda get-together. Why can't I have mine? What's the point of living in a big house if I never make use of it? And I can't remember ever having a birthday event at home. Hopefully, Maria will be cool with it. I won't be asking her to cook anything. McKay is looking after that department. This DJ Teaspoon brother is providing the music. All I have to do is make sure party folks don't get into Dad's garage.

Party thoughts filled my head as I left the classroom.

Maybe I should invite Wendy Reynolds. She'll be pissed if I don't. This might be a chance for us. Then again, it might not. None of her horses can come, though. I wonder who she'll come as?

I turned right into the corridor.

Oh shit!

Vincent Chapman and Donald Thompson.

There was a stand-off.

How did they know what classroom I was in? Was it just luck? Have they been stalking my ass?

Vincent glared at me as if I had dropped acid into his hair conditioner. 'Where's my ten-pound tax, Squire Boy?'

I didn't wait to discuss the issue. I scorched along the corridor. Chapman and Thompson hot-toed after me. 'Pay your taxes, Squire Boy!'

Where's my Crongton Knights when I need them? Where's a safe space? The library? Nah, too far away. I'm near reception. Headmaster's office is just around the corner. They won't give me the smack-down there.

I had no time to open exit doors. Chapman and Thompson were close behind as I burned along the hallway.

God! I'm soooo tired of this crap. Maybe I should come to school with my giant spade to defend myself.

'Squire Boy! Interest is going up tomorrow! Don't make this more difficult than you have to. Relax your pockets!'

I wished I had Jonah's speed. Other students had to get out of my way.

Take a left and then the next right.

I could almost feel Donald Thompson's breath on my neck as I screeched into the next corner.

Boof!

I crashed into the Christmas tree that stood in reception. It wobbled a bit before it fell.

Kablang!

I'm sure the whole school heard the sound it made as it bruised the floor. Baubles, tinsel and twigs were all around me. My legs got tangled up in the lights. I had knocked the angel clean off the tree and into the waiting area. Her arm was broken. I hoped God wouldn't want to give me a beatdown too. I wasn't sure if I was a bit dazed or if I was seeing real stars. I was able to focus enough to see the school administrator, Ms Simmonds, coming out of her office. The Christmas spirit wasn't with her.

'Do you know how long I worked on that?' she said. 'Hours and hours!'

Blazing daisies! There's Mr Foster too. The headteacher. My Christmas is double dead!

I glanced behind me. Chapman cursed my name and promised me a medieval death as he lifted a branch off himself. Thompson nursed some sort of knee injury.

'You're gonna pay for that!' he spat. 'I'm suing you! I'm taking you to the High Court.'

'In my office *now*!' ordered Mr Foster.

I followed Mr Foster into his office and sat as far away from Thompson and Chapman as I could.

Framed black-and-white photos of school hockey, football and basketball teams were on the walls. Classic English texts like *An Inspector Calls* and Shakespeare plays filled his bookshelves. Mr Foster parked behind this mega-desk that could've seated Jesus's disciples for the Last Supper. Propped up near his laptop was a framed photograph of some guy in winter garms posing with his skis. I guessed it was Mr Foster's partner. There was this rainbow-coloured mug with untold pens and pencils in it.

'Can you remember the first rule that you learned in Year Seven?' asked Mr Foster. He leaned forward and knitted his fingers together. He searched my eyes. He looked like he could do with one of Mum's last-minute-dot-com holidays. Tibet, Hawaii or somewhere.

'I dunno,' said Vincent Chapman. 'It's a long time ago.'

'Can't remember,' said Donald Thompson.

'Er . . . don't run along the corridors,' I said.

'And why is that?' Mr Foster asked.

Vincent Chapman and Donald Thompson swapped a baffled look.

'Because it can be dangerous and cause accidents,' I said.

'Correct!' Mr Foster nodded. 'So why, on the last day of term, did you three decide to use the corridors as if they were running tracks!'

'They were hunting me!' I replied. 'They wanted to give me a proper beat-down.'

'He ran into the back of me and started it all, sir,' said Vincent Chapman. 'I was minding my good business when Boy from the Hills crashed into me like a gone-wrong Jumbo. I don't know why he's starting on me. I haven't done him anything. He's a bit of a bully, sir. I'm scared of him.'

'Yeah,' Donald Thompson agreed. 'We haven't done him anything. He's definitely a bully. Always threatening to pollute us with his scarecrow hair.'

'Hmmmm.' Mr Foster scratched his nose. 'Hard to believe. How many times have you been inside my office this term?'

'None,' I replied. I looked around. 'It's bigger than I thought. Nice photos.'

Chapman and Thompson swapped another look. Mr Foster turned to them. 'And how many occasions have you two visited my office?'

Vincent started counting on his fingers.

'Five times!' Mr Foster raised his voice. 'Five times too many.'

'But this time it wasn't our fault,' argued Vincent. He pointed at me. 'He started it! He's got anger management issues. And he doesn't like poor people. This is a class issue.'

'They wanted to tax me,' I protested. '*They're* the bullies.'

'He knocked me over on purpose,' argued Vincent. 'And called me a peasant. Do you know how traumatising that is? My mum gets very up—'

'Enough! Enough!'

Mr Foster took a few breaths. He thought about it. He picked up a pen and twirled it between his fingers. 'Here's what you're going to do,' he said. 'You're going to pick up that tree and replace all the baubles and decorations before you go home. In silence!'

Timber!

'But I've gotta go shopping with my mum,' moaned Donald Thompson. 'I'm supposed to meet her on Crong Broadway. She's buying Grandad's Christmas present today. He's coming over for the holidays. He's very old – fifty-two.'

'I'm sure she'll wait for you,' said Mr Foster.

We went out to the reception area. Ms Simmonds had already replaced a few of the baubles.

'That's not necessary, Karen,' said Mr Foster. 'I have three willing volunteers who want to finish the job.'

As I replaced tinsel, baubles and other bits of Christmas decorations, Chapman and Thompson took turns in giving me ultimate death stares.

We had almost finished the job when this tall, mixed-race student approached me. Headphones covered his ears. His white shirt had escaped from his trousers. A fat tie bounced below his chin. A teaspoon rested in the breast pocket of his blazer. He wore lime-green Adidas trainers with yellow stripes. 'Are you Boy from the Hills?' he asked me.

'That's what they call me,' I replied.

'We call him Squire Boy,' chuckled Vincent Chapman.

'I'm DJ Teaspoon,' Mr Headphones said. 'Trust me! You won't be disappointed. I've got the banging beats and all the music you want for your party. I've even got an old-school turntable and a mixer in case anyone wants to spew any lyrics. It's gonna be mega-epic and legendary. Trust me, Crongton folk will be talking about this party when the world enters another ice age.'

Steep hills and ponds! I've had better days in this world.

Vincent Chapman dropped the string of tinsel he was about to place on a branch. 'You're having a party, Squire Boy? And you didn't invite me and Donald? *Scandalous!*'

'That's messed up,' said Donald. 'Look how long we've known you. And done stuff together.'

'Not polite,' Vincent added. 'Not polite at all.'

'All you've ever done is tax me!' I protested. 'You jacked my tablet on my first week at school! You tried to pull off my trainers. I could've reported that to the feds!'

'Tablet?' Chapman asked. 'What tablet?'

'Er . . . sorry I put you in a situation,' said DJ Teaspoon. 'All I want is a taxi ride to your gates to carry my equipment. Oh, and let me know the day.'

'Yeah.' Chapman nodded. 'When's the day?'

'It was just a rumour,' I said. 'There's no party. My folks wouldn't allow it anyway.'

'I heard they've gone away for a week and left you on your lonesome,' said DJ Teaspoon. 'That's what Venetia told me.'

I side-eyed DJ Teaspoon. *Shut the hell up!*

I hoped he got the message.

'You're lying!' accused Vincent. 'You're having a rave. Why wouldn't you invite me and Donald? We're two of the most popular brothers in the school. It's not a proper rave if we're not there.'

DJ Teaspoon offered me a knowing look.

'As I said, it's just a rumour. And even if I was having a

rave, I wouldn't invite you cos you would jack all the guests and stir-fry the local rabbits.'

Before Vincent could make a move on me, Mr Foster came out of his office. He inspected the tree. 'That'll do,' he said. 'Go on, go home. Have a merry Christmas.'

I headed right. Vincent and Donald were about to follow me.

'You two' – Mr Foster pointed at my tormentors – 'can leave by the north exit. I don't want to hear that you bumped into each other on the way home. Remember, you're still wearing South Crongton High blazers.'

'Dead man walking,' whispered Thompson. 'What do you want etched on your tombstone?'

'I heard that!' Mr Foster glared at Donald. 'I'm warning you two. No more trouble!'

4

Saira's Request

DJ Teaspoon stepped with me to the south exit. We didn't waste time.

'Trust me,' he said. 'I've got everything you need. You got Wi-Fi, right? Gotta couple of Bluetooth speakers. Can I come around before the party so I can scope the best place to set up my stuff?'

'Yeah,' I said. 'How about tomorrow morning?'

'I'm on for that,' he said. 'Give me your digits.'

I passed on my number. DJ Teaspoon sent me an instant message. His WhatsApp pic was an ancient vinyl record. 'I'm not gonna let you down,' he said. 'It's gonna be an Afrobeat explosion. That's what's killing it right now. Everyone's gonna be bubbling.'

'I'm sure they will be,' I replied.

Saira's Request

'Oh, one last thing,' DJ Teaspoon said. 'Can I bring an assistant?'

'An assistant?' I repeated.

'Yeah, her name's Mellow Enchanter. She'll fill in when I need a break or something.'

'OK,' I agreed. 'But that's all. I don't want no friends of friends or second and third cousins.'

'I can sign up for that,' said DJ Teaspoon. 'Trust me, Boy from the Hills, South Crong town-hall folk are gonna put up a plaque on the wall of your house that's gonna read: *Here is the site where Boy from the Hills hosted his legendary party.*'

Waiting for me at the south exit was Saira.

She's never hung around for me after school before. Maybe she can't come to my rave and wants to spill that breaking news in person.

She gave me a wave.

'Where have you been?' Saira asked. 'Been waiting ages. And I dinged you. Why didn't you pick up?'

I checked my phone. Four missed calls.

'Sorry,' I replied. 'Still have it on silent. You know, school rules and all that.'

'What kept you?' she pressed again.

We set off in the direction of Crongton Heath. I checked over my shoulder to see if Chapman and Thompson were following. They weren't.

33

Relief!

It was getting dark. Streetlights flickered on. *I gotta walk Bossi soon.*

'Chapman and Thompson kept me,' I replied. 'They were waiting for me outside my maths class. As usual, they wanted to tax me. I had to jet away from them. Was sonic booming towards reception and ka-blammed into the Christmas tree. Knocked it over. Things went flying. For a second or two, I was in a Christmas-tree world. Foster came out of his office. He didn't give me a round of applause.'

'So, you got detention?' Saira asked.

'Yep. Had to clear up the mess with Chapman and Thompson. It wasn't joy to all men.'

'Sorry to hear,' Saira said. 'Them two need locking up.'

'And flinging away the key to a distant galaxy.'

Saira chuckled.

'What is it?' I asked. 'I don't usually get company on my trod home.'

'Your party,' replied Saira.

'What about it?'

'Can . . . can I bring someone?'

'Yeah, course.' I nodded. 'Who?'

'Merlene Quarrie.'

'Merlene Quarrie?' I repeated. 'The track runner?'

'Yep,' Saira said. 'We haven't had a proper date yet. And . . . and not too many school folks know about us. It'll be like our coming-out thing.'

'It's gonna be fancy dress,' I reminded her. 'Juniper's idea. Any idea who you might come as?'

Saira stopped walking. She smiled. 'That's a good question,' she said. 'I'll check out what they've got at the Crongton Party Exchange. You better get your ass down there too. All the good stuff is taken early at this time of year.'

'Maybe we can skip there on Sunday,' I said. 'After church.'

'Yeah,' Saira agreed. 'I'm on that. It's gonna feel a bit strange for me going to church. But it's to support Venetia.'

'Church is not my usual hangout,' I said. 'But Venetia needs our love.'

'Oh, one warning,' Saira said. 'Don't even think about coming as Black Panther. Jonah and Liccle Bit are already beefing about that one.'

'Black Panther? Me? Nah, that's the longest thing from my mind. I'm the wrong colour for starters.'

Saira laughed. She always tipped her head back when she did that. 'You're too funny.'

'I try.'

'OK,' said Saira. 'Thanks for letting me invite Merlene. I'm really looking forward to it. You deserve a party.'

We said our goodbyes and I headed towards the Heath. I still had to get the greenlight from Maria.

5

There's Something
I Didn't Know About Maria

I reached home to find Maria draining spaghetti to add to the Bolognese she had just cooked. I didn't know what spices she had put in the dish, but my nostrils loved it.

'Hi, Maria,' I greeted. 'How was your day? Where's Bossi?'

'Day was OK,' she said. 'Do you want to eat now? Bossi is downstairs in the basement.'

I went downstairs and checked on Bossi. He was asleep beneath the pool table.

Chapman and Thompson wouldn't trouble me if they knew Bossi was my guard dog.

I came back up and sat at the dining table. Maria served my dinner and her own. I sprinkled some grated cheese on top. Maria's eyes looked puffy. She twirled the spaghetti around her fork but didn't put it into her mouth. Her thoughts were in another postcode.

There's Something I Didn't Know About Maria

'Something up?' I asked.

'Eat your dinner before it gets cold,' she replied.

I sunk a mouthful. Maria stared at her plate.

'Are you sure you're OK?' I pressed.

She placed her fork on her plate before she looked up to me. She wiped her mouth with a kitchen towel. 'Crisanto won't be coming back until New Year's Day,' she said.

'New Year's Day?' I repeated. 'I thought you said you'll be seeing him Christmas Eve?'

Maria stood up. She took a couple of breaths as if she was deciding to spill something big. 'That's what he told me!' She raised her voice. 'We'll spend Christmas week together. He promised he wouldn't accept any overtime or take on another cruise. And then he texts me today to tell me he's been offered time-and-a-half.'

'Sor-sorry to hear,' I managed.

'He said it'll go towards our wedding,' Maria went on. 'Right now, I just want to see him. It's been four months! And he promised me!'

'You . . . you can stay with us over Christmas,' I suggested. 'Better than being on your lonesome. I'm sure it'll be cool with my parents.'

'With respect,' Maria said, placing her hands on her hips, 'I don't want to spend Christmas with my employers. I like you . . . but . . .'

'I get it,' I said. 'You wanna spend Christmas with someone you love, right?'

'Yes! Yes! You understand. Every day I come here. I clean,

I cook, I speak to your parents, I speak to you. I'm even cooking for a dog now. But I have my own life.'

'Did . . . did you tell Crisanto how you feel?' I asked.

Maria sat back down. She fingered her engagement ring. 'I've been engaged three years! Sometimes I think I'll never get married.'

'You will, you will,' I replied. 'Crisanto will be cadazy not to marry you.'

She ate two mouthfuls of Bolognese. 'I was a bit rude,' she admitted.

'How rude?'

Suddenly, Maria giggled. 'I can't tell you,' she said. 'You're a minor.'

'Trust me,' I replied. 'I go to South Crong High. I've heard X-rated swear words that gangster rappers would cry and complain about.'

Maria laughed again. She composed herself. 'I told him in a voicemail that he'd rather make love to a cruise ship's funnel than his beautiful fiancée at home.'

This time I had an attack of the giggles.

'Excuse me,' she said. 'Just going to get something to go with my dinner.'

She found a mortice key on her keyring, smiled, and went downstairs to the basement.

Is she going to the wine cellar?

Three minutes later, she came back up clutching a bottle of champagne. Gold foil wrapped the top half of it. It wasn't a small bottle.

'That's . . . that's one of Mum's expensive bottles,' I said.

'She won't miss it,' she replied. 'There's plenty down there.' Maria got herself a glass from a cabinet. 'It's a shame you can't share a drink with me,' she said. 'But I need to go to bed with something tonight, if it's not Crisanto. Damn him and his bloody big cruise ships.'

'I hope Mum doesn't notice,' I said.

'She won't notice from you because I'm cooking all the dog's dinners,' Maria said. 'When you take him for a walk, whatever you do, don't take him near the duck pond. He'll think it's dinner time. I'm surprised he doesn't quack instead of bark.'

'Can I ask you something, Maria?'

Maria poured herself a full glass. She took a sip. 'Aaaaaahhhh. That's better. Quality stuff! I do enjoy the perks of my job. What do you want to ask me?'

'Is it all right if I have a party?'

'Yes, of course,' Maria replied. 'It's your house. No champagne though. When are you going to have it?'

'Er . . . after the weekend. Maybe Tuesday.'

'Yes, go on, enjoy yourself. Why should the two of us be miserable over Christmas time? Your parents have abandoned you. Again! And here I am, waiting for a man who's always away. Again! We make a right pair.'

'You sure?'

'Course I'm sure! Live it up! But no drinking. I don't want to be responsible for drunk kids walking about on the Heath or in the woods. You know what they're like around here.'

I finished my dinner, washed up my plate and left Maria sipping her champagne. She looked well sad. I didn't know what to say to her.

I made my way upstairs to my room. I sat on my king-size bed and stared at the framed landscape photographs that hung on my walls. There was this one aerial shot of a loch in Scotland. Well pretty. Another was of a fjord in Sweden. My favourite was probably the one of the Amazon cutting through the Brazilian rainforest, taken from above. It had this beautiful rich green to it. They all brought me calm.

I changed into my jeans, boots and the Christmas jumper that Mum bought me last year and woke up Bossi for his walk. Before I reached the front door, someone slapped the letter box.

6

Captain Heath

I opened my door. Standing in front of me was Wendy Reynolds, holding the reins of one of her horses. It was a big brown thing with flecks of white on his face. He had long eyelashes and a tail that I guessed Wendy had braided.

Bossi got a bit excited and jumped around a bit at the sight of the horse. Maybe he thought he could mate with it.

Be cool. Be cool, I said to myself.

'This is Captain Heath. What is that?' Wendy asked.

'Mrs Utili's dog,' I replied. 'Bossi. I was about to take him for his evening trod. I'd have asked you to come but I have no idea where he's gonna take me. He's strong enough to pull the nine-fifty-four train from Crongton to Spenge.'

Wendy smiled. 'What are you doing with Mrs Utili's dog?'

'She's gone to Salzburg to spend a Mozart Christmas,' I replied. 'Guess who's got the short straw?'

A Crongton Christmas Party

'I haven't seen you lately,' Wendy said. 'Apart from dog-sitting, what you got planned for the Christmas holidays?'

Bossi pulled me towards the woods. Wendy followed with Captain Heath. He was much better behaved than Bossi. Bossi yanked off my arm, sniffed, farted and did his business.

'Believe it or not,' I said. 'I'm having a party.'

'A party!' repeated Wendy. She clapped her hands. 'That's brilliant. When? What made you think about having a party?'

'One of my friends at school,' I replied. 'The Tuesday before Christmas. At first I thought, nah, but to hell with it – my parents have gone to the Highlands.'

'Scotland?'

'Yep. They're on some campaign against grimy lakes and rivers.'

'Again? A week before Christmas?'

'The more I think about it, the more I believe I deserve a rave,' I said.

'How exciting.'

'It's fancy dress,' I said.

'Oh, that's easy. I'll come as Rachael Blackmore.'

'Who's she?' I asked.

Suddenly, Bossi got interested in another dog. It was an Alsatian. I held on to the lead with all my might. *Splat!* I ended up on the ground. Wendy helped me calm Bossi down. The Alsatian ran away. Bossi barked after it. Captain Heath looked on. He wasn't impressed.

Captain Heath

Maybe I should just let him run around. It'll be less embarrassing.

'Thanks,' I said. 'Lakes and hills, he's strong. Anyway, Rachael who?'

We resumed walking. I didn't want Wendy to know that my arm was quite possibly pulled out of its socket. I probably needed urgent medical attention.

'Blackmore,' she replied. 'The Irish jockey.'

'Never heard of her. As you know, horse racing's not my thing.'

Wendy slapped me on the head. 'Never heard of Rachael Blackmore? Don't you listen to anything I tell you? Where have you been? She won the Grand National and the Gold Cup. The first woman in history to do so.'

'You're gonna come as a jockey?'

'Why not?' said Wendy. 'What about you?'

'I haven't really thought about it,' I admitted. 'Maybe Robin Hood.'

Wendy stopped walking and bust out a mega-laugh. 'Robin Hood! Robin Hood! He stole from the rich and gave to the poor. What are you gonna do? Steal from the rich and give to yourself. Ha ha ha ha!'

I swear even Captain Heath laughed. He nodded three times and made some kinda giggling sound. Bossi took no interest. He sniffed a tree stump and pissed against it.

I was quite offended. When I was little, Uncle Stuey told me great tales about Robin Hood, Little John and Friar Tuck. I once asked Dad to take me on a trip to Sherwood Forest. I was proper serious, but Dad just laughed.

'Mind you,' Wendy said. 'Robin Hood dancing with Rachael Blackmore would be a cool sight to behold.'

'Dance?' I replied. 'I can't dance. I can't even walk properly.'

'I'll lead you.'

'No, no, no,' I said. 'It'll be embarrassing. All my friends are gonna be there.'

Wendy pulled a face. 'Even our colours will match,' she said. 'Me in a green-and-yellow stripey top and you in your green shirt and little hat.'

'I still can't dance.'

Wendy smiled. 'We'll have to do something about that.'

I wanted to change the subject. Quickly.

'How are things at Joan Benson?' I asked.

'School? Hate it. If you don't watch *Love Island*, wear make-up or have a Coach handbag, you're an outcast. No one wants to make friends with a girl who scoops horse shit and cleans out stables every morning. Some of them call me Madame Manure. My parents pay a lot of money for it, so I don't complain to them too much.'

'Sorry to hear,' I said. 'I know what it's like to be the outsider. First few weeks of South Crong High were a living nightmare.'

'Yeah, I remember,' Wendy replied. 'Still don't know why your parents sent you there. They had the money—'

'I think Bossi's big enough to have his own stable,' I cut in. 'Your dad taking on any extra animals for the holidays?'

Captain Heath

Wendy laughed. 'No, eight horses are enough to be looking after. There's a lot of horse crap to be scooped out every morning as it is.'

'Captain Heath,' I said. 'Will he be racing soon?'

'On Boxing Day.' Wendy smiled. 'At Sandown over the hurdles. It's a two-miler. My dad says he has a brilliant chance.'

'Shame you can't bet on him.'

Wendy half-grinned and side-eyed me. 'There are ways around that.'

We walked for a while in silence following the path through the woods. It was proper dark. Owls did their thing. Smaller animals quick-toed here and there.

'Doesn't . . . doesn't it bother you that your parents are away so much?' Wendy asked.

'They say I've got everything I need,' I replied.

'Apart from their presence in your life. What's more important? You or their stupid campaigns? Sorry to bring this up again, but you need to talk to them.'

'I will,' I said. 'When they get back.'

'That's what you said last time.'

'This time I will.'

'Hmmmm.'

'Let me get the party out of the way first,' I said. 'Never hosted anything before.'

'You got someone to play the music?'

'Yep. Some bruv at school. DJ Teaspoon. He's doing it for free.'

'What about food?'

'Oh, that's in safe hands,' I replied. 'That'll be my good friend McKay. He takes his food very, very seriously. He's always clashing with the school dinner folks. He's gonna bake some chicken rolls, Jamaican patties and mince pies.'

'Sounds like you've got it all sorted,' Wendy said. 'On Monday I'll come around and we can have a practice dance.'

'A practice dance?'

'Yeah.' Wendy smiled. 'You don't want to look stupid in front of your friends.'

Hollering hedges! How do I get out of this one? Wendy's pretty and all, but I wasn't wrong when I said I can't dance. Maybe I'll ask Venetia to teach me? No, Liccle Bit might think that I'm making a move on her. This is gonna go all wrong.

She walked me to my gates before we said our goodbyes. Bossi had made a new friend with Captain Heath. I just hoped he realised that he is a horse.

'Don't forget Monday!' called out Wendy.

'I won't.'

Captain Heath swished his tail and did a crap.

Maybe he's trying to tell me something.

I was getting more worries about Monday than the actual party.

7

DJ Teaspoon and the DB5

I headed home, cleaned Bossi's paws with kitchen paper, and made my way upstairs. Bossi followed me and jumped on my bed. He nearly broke it.

I sat down at my desk and switched on my laptop, where I had been designing this garden. I soon realised that I hadn't heard anything from Maria. I stepped into the hallway and tickled her door. No response.

'Maria? Everything all right?'

Still nothing.

What to do? What to do? Am I invading her space by entering her bedroom? She did look proper upset before I took Bossi for his evening trod.

I opened the door. The curtains were still open. Propped up on her bedside cabinet was a framed photograph of her and Crisanto on a trip to Paris. Cheek to cheek, they looked in love. The Eiffel Tower was in the background. The bottle of champagne resting on her dressing table was half-empty. Nothing was in the glass.

There she was. Sprawled out on top of her bed.

I found a blanket at the bottom of her wardrobe and covered her with it.

The next morning, Bossi woke me just before six. He basically booted me out of bed. I made myself porridge for breakfast. Maria had been up before me. She had duck meat boiling away on the cooker.

I took Bossi for a short walk on the Heath after he had gobbled up his meal. There was no drama until he spotted this Labrador. Bossi chased after it and, before my eyes, the Labrador turned into a greyhound.

By the time I got back, I had received over thirty WhatsApp messages. Venetia and Saira wanted to know which day I was hosting the party. McKay wanted funds for his party shopping. Liccle Bit and Jonah were having a WhatsApp beef about who would look best in a Black Panther outfit and Juniper suggested a party game that involved ferrets, hamsters and gerbils. A sort of pass-the-parcel thing.

What on God's good green earth could that be?

I texted back saying Tuesday was the day. Everyone sent me a thumbs-up.

PARTY TIME!

DJ Teaspoon and the DB5

Juniper still wanted to know about her animal pass-the-parcel game. I replied that animal charities might not love it. McKay messaged that he'd be coming around with DJ Teaspoon around 10 a.m. I sent a group message.

> Please don't leak news about my rave to Chapman and Thompson. I don't want them two to know where I live.

My gates were smacked at 10.15 a.m. McKay had come with DJ Teaspoon. He entered and looked around my house like he had stepped into another dimension.

'Your place is mega-normous!' he said. 'Your dinner table is bigger than my bedroom. You could hold your rave inside your pantry. Your dad's not the number one supplier of dragon hip pills in the UK, is he?'

'No, he's a barrister.'

'A barrister? Them folks who wear white wigs?'

'Yep.'

'And you get mega dollars for doing that?'

'Yep.'

I offered them a glass of orange juice before I took them downstairs to the basement.

'Man!' said DJ Teaspoon. 'You got a pool table! If I knew that, I would've been your bredren from day dot. No offence.'

'That's good to know,' I said.

Where was Bossi? He had been sleeping under the pool table.

'Excuse me for a sec,' I said. 'Just wanna check on the dog.'

A Crongton Christmas Party

I went upstairs and found Bossi in my bedroom. When I returned to the basement, McKay and DJ Teaspoon were playing a game of pool. Bossi had decided to follow me.

'God save my lyrics!' DJ Teaspoon raised his voice. 'What's that!'

DJ Teaspoon retreated from the pool table and held his cue in such a way to defend himself.

'That's Bossi,' I replied. 'He's harmless.'

'What is it?' DJ Teaspoon pressed.

'A neighbour's dog.'

'That's no dog! That's the bastard kid of a lion and a bear.'

McKay laughed. Bossi wasn't impressed.

'It's not gonna be around during the party is it?' DJ Teaspoon asked. 'I don't want that thing getting in the way of my mixing.'

'No,' I said. 'He'll be in the back garden.'

'Good thinking, good thinking.' DJ Teaspoon nodded. 'You don't want that lion-grizzly thing feasting on your guests.'

Bossi sniffed a leg of the pool table before making himself comfortable beneath it.

'He's gentle,' I said.

'I hope so.'

'Anyway,' I changed the subject. 'The party will be down here. Just got to move the pool table into the cinema room.'

'You've got a cinema room?' DJ Teaspoon asked. 'I

DJ Teaspoon and the DB5

should've definitely made your acquaintance in Year Seven. Have you got all the *James Bond* and *Mission: Impossible* movies? Never seen 'em on a big screen. Only on the small TV we've got at home.'

'Got a few,' I replied.

McKay and DJ Teaspoon resumed their game. McKay grinned as he potted the black ball. DJ Teaspoon placed his cue on the table. 'Is it true that your pops has a DB5?'

'Er . . . who told you that?' I glanced at McKay. He stared at the floor.

'It's no hype?' DJ Teaspoon pressed.

'Er . . . yeah . . . but he doesn't drive it. He spends most of his time polishing it.'

'Can I see it?' urged DJ Teaspoon. 'I've never scoped one up close live and direct. Please? Trust me, I won't even breathe on it. Just wanna see it. Been a fan of *James Bond* for the longest time. Fave movie is *Casino Royale* where Bond wins the car in a card game. And that girl on the horse on the beach! *Man!* My heart starts walloping. Oh, and the airport scene. That's the bomb.'

'My pops says I can't let anyone into the garage,' I said.

'Told you,' said McKay to DJ Teaspoon.

'But he's missing,' said DJ Teaspoon. '*He* zoomed up to Scotland and left you on your lonesome. Come on, Boy from the Hills. I just wanna see some car candy. I'm not Superman. I haven't got X-ray vision that could burn a line into the paintwork. And I ain't got dragon breath either. Remember, I'm DJing your rave for free.'

McKay set up the balls for another game of pool. DJ Teaspoon stared at me with big eyes. He played the opening shot, splitting the balls apart. McKay potted a few balls and was about to win the game.

'DB5?' DJ Teaspoon urged again. 'No one else needs to know.'

Can't do too much harm if he just has a look.

'OK,' I agreed. 'But no selfies and no standing on the bonnet.'

'As if I would do such a thing!' DJ Teaspoon replied.

Dad kept a spare key to the garage in his wardrobe. He thought I didn't know, but I had seen him go in there when he had his bougie friends around. His fave Bond was Sean Connery. In second place was Daniel Craig. He didn't have much love for Roger Moore.

I felt a dose of guilt as I collected the keys from a chrome hook. I led McKay and DJ Teaspoon out the front and to the garage. Bossi followed us. DJ Teaspoon stopped in his tracks to check out the garden.

'You get a gardener to shave your hedges and trim your little trees?' he asked.

'Nah,' I replied. 'I do it myself. It's my hobby. I look after the back garden too.'

'So that's why you come to school with half of the world's grass in your hair.'

I had to laugh. I opened the double-doors to the garage and switched on a wall light. Every item had been placed on a shelf and in its right place. It was tidier than my bedroom. I sniffed car wax. The DB5 shone like a new ride hot off the production line. Dad had also replaced the tyres on the wheels.

'Oh, my sweet mixes!' DJ Teaspoon raised his voice. 'So, it wasn't hype. Check out the bodywork! And it's grey-silverish just like the one in the *James Bond* movies.'

DJ Teaspoon ran his hands over the body of the DB5. He peered through the windscreen. 'I don't suppose you got the keys so I can sit in it?' he asked.

'Nope,' I replied. 'Don't know where my pops keeps those.'

'It's . . . it's magnifi-locious!' DJ Teaspoon shouted. 'Trust me, one day, I'm gonna be driving one of them speed fiends. I've made a new friend.'

'A new friend?' McKay laughed. 'You can't dance with it. It won't be allowed to gain entrance at the movies, and it probably doesn't like wearing fancy dress.'

'I bet you were showing it nuff love the first time you saw it,' said DJ Teaspoon.

'Can we go shopping now?' asked McKay. 'We need to get the decorations, food and stuff.'

'Decorations?' I repeated.

'Yeah,' McKay said. 'Can't have a rave without decorations. Even your T-Rex will have to wear a party hat.'

'Bossi's not a dinosaur,' I replied. 'He's a dog.'

DJ Teaspoon shook his head. 'If that thing's a dog, then I'm a dragon.'

'You're not wrong with that breath,' joked McKay.

I double-checked that I had locked the garage door before returning the key to Dad's wardrobe.

On the way to the South Crong Aztec superstore, DJ Teaspoon told us how one day he was gonna play beats on holiday islands like Ibiza and Bali. We said goodbye to him on Crong Broadway.

'He's not gonna broadcast to the whole of Crongton that I'm having a rave, is he?' I fretted.

'Nah,' McKay replied. 'He's not like that. But if he does make it big, I wanna free squeeze to any gig he plays at.'

McKay collected all the soft drinks and ingredients we needed for the chicken and Jamaican patties. He seemed to know what he was looking for. Just as we joined the checkout queue, he spotted someone who attended our school.

'Isn't that Ava Cohen?' he wondered.

He pointed to an aisle about thirty metres away from us. I concentrated my eyes. 'Yes, that's her.'

'Can I invite her to your Christmas party?' McKay asked.

'She probably won't come,' I replied. 'She's Jewish. Remember?'

'I wanna ask her anyway,' said McKay.

He had the look of a hungry hound about him. 'Jews don't celebrate Christmas,' I said.

'We're not really celebrating Christmas,' McKay argued.

'I've got three Christmas trees in my house,' I reminded him. 'And we've just bought untold balloons, party hats, mince pies and tinsel.'

'That might be a deal-breaker,' McKay said. 'But it might not be. She's pretty, man. And she's the queen of angles. At the very least, if I get on the good side of her, I'll get help with my maths homework.'

The cashier was ready to scan our groceries. I placed our stuff on the conveyor belt as McKay scoped Ava Cohen, wondering how to approach her.

When I paid for the shopping, McKay sucked in a long breath, let it out, and marched over to Ava.

'Be my wingman,' he said.

'What does a wingman do?' I asked.

'Make me look good.'

'How?'

'Go with the flow.'

'You haven't got any flow.'

'Just follow me.'

'To the embarrassment zone?' I joked.

I shook my head. *This is not gonna end well.*

'Ava, Ava!' McKay greeted. 'How's tings?'

'Oh, hi, McKay. Things are OK. Just getting some holiday shopping done.'

'I'm sooooo glad I bounced into you,' said McKay. He slapped me on the shoulder and grinned a wide grin. 'My man here, Boy from the Hills, one of the most popular brothers in our year . . .'

'He is?' Ava glanced at me, clearly wondering who the hell I was. I felt proper ridiculous.

'Anyway,' continued McKay. 'He's having a Christmas rave.'

'I . . . I don't really do Christmas,' said Ava.

'It's not really a Christmas ting,' said McKay. 'It's just that time of year. It's fancy dress. And of course, we'd like you to come.'

McKay nudged me in the back.

'Yes, we definitely want you to come,' I said.

'You're on our A-list,' added McKay.

'When is it?' Ava wanted to know.

'Tuesday,' I replied.

'If I was on your A-list,' Ava queried. 'How comes I'm only finding out about it now?'

'It was a last-minute-dot-com thing,' said McKay. 'Security reasons. We didn't want bad breeds like Vincent Chapman and Donald Thompson finding out. And I don't have your phone number, hint, hint!'

Ava thought about it. 'I . . . I don't know. As I said, I don't really do Christmas parties.'

'Trust me,' McKay cut in. 'They'll be no baby in a manger. No Three Wise Men, no frankincense, gold or that other thing. No shepherds, no sheep and no donkeys. And it definitely won't be a silent night.'

Ava laughed. McKay wasn't wrong. She was well pretty. She had big dark eyes and a tiny silver stud in her nose.

'It doesn't give me a lot of time to find an outfit,' Ava said.

'Come as Einstein,' McKay suggested. 'Just like you, he had top-ratings at maths.'

'I'm . . . I'm not sure.'

'Boy from the Hills!' McKay urged. 'Give Ava your address.'

I scribbled down my location on the back of my shopping receipt and handed it to Ava.

'You live on Crongton Heath?' Ava asked.

'He certainly does,' replied McKay. 'So, they'll be none of that crushy, squashy business like a party in the estate. He lives in the palace with the circular gravel driveway. Tings are gonna boot off about six.'

'OK.' Ava nodded.

'I *don't* live in a palace!' I said.

'You live in a proper palace,' McKay laughed. 'Even the King would get lost in your place.'

'He's over the top,' I said to Ava.

'So, are you gonna come?' McKay asked.

'I'll . . . I'll think about it,' Ava replied.

We left Ava to pack her shopping. Once we were outside, McKay asked, 'Do you think she'll come?'

'Don't know,' I said. 'We'll find out on the night.'

'We definitely will,' said McKay. 'I'm gonna remind DJ Teaspoon to make sure he plays some slow songs. Have you got someone special you wanna invite?'

I thought of Wendy Reynolds. I think I blushed.

'There is, isn't there!' said McKay. 'Do I know her?'

'Yeah, think you met her twice.'

'Oh, I know, it's that horse girl! I always said she's on you. Have you invited her yet? What's her name again?'

'Wendy,' I replied. 'And yes, I've already invited her.'

'Cool. Hopefully, we'll all have someone to dance with when the slow tunes are bubbling.'

You can't dance, my brain told my feet.

We hailed a taxi to get the shopping home and played one more game of pool before he helped me move the pool table.

'This party's gonna be massive,' said McKay. 'Everyone's gonna be chatting about it for the longest time.'

'I'm not sure if that's a good thing,' I said. 'Anyway, gotta take Bossi out for his late afternoon trod before I step to the Crongton movie house.'

'Oh, I nearly forgot,' said McKay. 'I've got to zoom home, deal with my armpits and put on something fresh. You never knew who you might meet at the movies. What are we watching again?'

'*A Black and White Christmas,*' I reminded him. 'It's about a white girl who invites this homeless black bruv to her family Christmas dinner. Turns out he's richer than the white family. Much richer. It's a romcom.'

'Sounds proper soppy,' said McKay.

'Blame Liccle Bit and Venetia.'

8

Party Crashers at Barrington's Diner

I fell asleep halfway through the movie. Needless to say, the black bruv and the white girl smacked lips at the end. McKay had to nudge me awake when the credits rolled. Saira had tears in her eyes. Liccle Bit had his arm around Venetia for the entire film. I wondered if Wendy might go for a date night at the movies.

Probably not, unless it's about a horse or that jockey she was rapping about.

We left the cinema and headed on to Crong Broadway. It was just after 9.30 p.m. The street was busy. The Christmas lights above us looked well pretty. There was a long queue outside Hamza's Kebab Takeaway. A Father Christmas slept in a shop doorway with empty cans of beer around him. There was an argument booting off at the Crongton Town House pub. It was packed with drinkers. Someone sang Wizzard's *I Wish It Could Be Christmas Every Day* at the end of the street. It wasn't in tune.

'What a bad ending!' Juniper said. 'At one point I thought they were gonna kill off the black bruv. You know, give him some incurable disease. And then I expected him to leave all his millions to homeless hamsters and gerbils. That would've made it interesting.'

'Juniper,' I said. 'What's with you and hamsters and gerbils this week? Last week it was sharks and giant squids.'

'I felt sorry for them watching this doc where a snake feasted on them,' she replied. 'It slowly digested 'em over many days and you could see the hamster-size bulge in its neck.'

'Eeeeew! Gross!' said Venetia.

I think we all wanted to change the subject.

'It was better than I expected,' said Jonah. 'The twist was good. Wasn't expecting the black bruv to be an heir to a mega fortune. Man! What would I spend all that money on!'

McKay pointed to Jonah's head. 'Haircuts,' he replied. 'You definitely need to invest.'

'Screw you!' spat back Jonah.

'It wasn't just about money,' said Saira. She wiped a tear from her eye. 'He wanted someone to love him for himself. All the girls he met before were only interested in his money. That's why he pretended to be homeless. It was sweet.'

'How can you not invite me?' Kiran asked. 'Outrageous! Didn't I back you up in Year Eight when Vincent Chapman fired off wet paper pellets to your head?'

He wasn't wrong. Chapman had these long elastic bands and used them to launch soggy-paper ammo at me whenever the teacher wasn't looking. I had red marks all over my neck. When I reached home, Mum thought I had the measles.

'Where did you hear that Boy from the Hills was having a rave?' asked Jonah.

Kiran grinned. 'I have my sources.'

'DJ Teaspoon?' I guessed.

'Let him come,' said Juniper. She smiled a trouble-making smile. 'On one condition. He must save one dance with me.'

Caroline Stringer wasn't laughing. She side-eyed Juniper like she wanted to club her with something spiky.

'What you gonna come as?' Venetia asked.

'Not sure yet,' replied Kiran. 'But I promise you, it'll be Christmassy.'

'I haven't said yes yet,' I protested.

'Let him come,' said McKay. 'At least he's no friend to Chapman and Thompson.'

This party's getting too big. If Kiran Cassidy knows about it, who else does? Triple-jumping tadpoles! My whole year might know.

'I'm not sure,' I said.

'He did help our basketball team beat the North Crong,'

said Liccle Bit. 'His last shot won the game. And we all celebrated like it was 2199. You can't deny that he's a legend.'

'That was a sweet moment.' Jonah nodded. 'He was carried off the court shoulder-high.'

'Folks were chanting his name,' added Liccle Bit.

'Yes, they were,' recalled Juniper. She gazed at Kiran. 'You looked soooo good in your kit. But I preferred your hair when you had the wild-Afro look. Can't you grow it like that again.'

Kiran ignored Juniper. Instead, he waited for my response.

'Oh, OK.' I nodded. 'But no plus ones or twos.'

'What about me?' Caroline complained. 'I'm Kiran's girlfriend.'

'OK,' I said. 'But no distant cousins.'

'Agreed.' Kiran smiled.

Kiran grabbed Caroline's hand and led her over to the counter. Juniper gave Caroline a murderous side-eye. 'Can't see what he sees in her,' she said.

'Captain of our netball team,' Saira said. 'She also runs over the hurdles, flings the javelin and is the first girl off in the relay team.'

'She's well versatile,' added Jonah. 'They're training her to be a heptathlete. Mr Smallwood reckons that if she works hard, she'll make it to the Olympics.'

'I could make the Olympics too,' said Juniper. 'If they did graveyard sleeping as an event.'

'She even took part in this year's school play,' said Venetia.

'But can she defend herself and Kiran if they accidentally fell into the lion's den at the zoo at feeding time?' said Juniper. 'That's the ultimate test.'

None of us knew how to answer that.

'You fancy him, don't you, Juniper?' I asked.

'Fancy Kiran Cassidy?' Juniper pulled a face. She thought about it. 'He might have a chance with me if he wasn't so vain. I don't like a man who spends more time fixing his fat school tie than I do.'

Everyone laughed.

'Are you all prepped and ready to go to church in the morning?' McKay asked Venetia.

'I'm a bit nervous,' Venetia admitted. 'Never sang in front of adults before. Never sang a solo in church before either.'

'She's gonna whack that ball outta the park,' Liccle Bit said. 'Nothing to worry about. They do allow you to film stuff in church, don't they?'

'Er . . . I'm not sure,' replied Venetia.

'We'll all be there to holler for you,' said Saira.

'Then after that we'll step down to the Crongton Party Exchange to get our outfits,' I reminded everyone.

'I've already got mine.' Saira smiled.

'What is it?' I was a little hurt Saira had been without me.

'You'll find out on the night.'

'And I've already got mine,' said Venetia. 'I'll give you a clue. It's sporty. Not even Liccle Bit knows.'

'She won't tell me,' moaned Liccle Bit.

'It all adds to the excitement of the night.' Venetia grinned. 'Oh, try not to be late tomorrow morning. Service starts at 9.30 a.m.'

Everyone stared at Juniper.

'I'm *never* late!' she protested. 'That's an outrageous accusation.'

Ten minutes later, we said our goodbyes.

The house was very quiet when I arrived home. I started up the stairs and must have woken Bossi. He jumped up the staircase and made himself comfortable on the carpet near the foot of my bed. I think he might have missed me.

Kinda nice to have someone missing you, even if it's a dog.

9

Checking In With Mum and Dad

I changed into my pyjamas. Before I crashed, I checked my phone. There were three missed calls from Mum.

Better call before I snooze out.

'Hi, Mum. How's the Highlands?'

'Don't give me "How's the Highlands". Why don't you ever answer your phone?'

'I was at the movies. It was on silent.'

'Hmmm. You could've messaged me.'

'While I'm watching a movie?'

'Are you taking Bossi for his walks?'

'Yes, morning and early evening.'

'Good, good. Are you going to have one or two friends over for a movie night?'

'Er . . . yes . . . you could call it that. On Tuesday.'

'That's very nice,' said Mum. 'Maybe you can share a

pizza or something. You've got the money for that. Your father downloaded a few new films on to the hard drive. They're all age appropriate. Keep the basement tidy and make sure no one rips the pool table. Your father just got a new cloth laid. Use that new hoover attachment on the furniture.'

'I'll be tidy, Mum, and I'll be careful.'

'And no taking your friends to the garage,' she warned. 'You know how your father feels about that precious car of his.'

'Mum, I don't even know where the key is.'

'And if you're going to church, make sure you wash your hair,' Mum said. 'I've got a few friends who attend that church. I don't want them seeing you turn up in a state.'

'Mum, I was planning to wash my hair. Is there anything else?'

Mum thought about it. 'Just that we wish you were here with us.'

'With you? Campaigning in cold soggy lands about how they're polluting a lake? Not my thing, Mum.'

'You'll learn,' Mum replied. 'We're doing it all for you. The young. One day you'll thank us.'

'One day you and Dad might hang around long enough for me to thank you.'

'No need to be sarcastic, Colin,' replied Mum. 'We're here for a good cause. What's the point of making good money if you can't help decent people and good causes?'

I couldn't answer that one.

Checking In With Mum and Dad

'Mum, I'm tired,' I said. 'We'll chat tomorrow. Got to get up early to take Bossi for his trod and then get prepped for church.'

'Don't forget to polish your shoes!'

'Mum! I'm not a kid.'

'And wear one of your nice jackets and ties.'

'Mum!'

Gosh. She's like a sergeant for the must-look-respectable feds. Why does she care how I look? She's never here to see me.

10

Venetia's Challenge

Sunday morning. Two days before party time.

Bossi was hyper on his walk. He spotted an Afghan Hound and hot-pawed after it. I tried to hang on, but I dropped the lead.

By the time I had caught up to Bossi, he had done something... unpleasant.

'Disgusting!' said the Afghan Hound's owner. She wore a cream-coloured rain mac and black wellington boots.

Bossi was trying to hump the female mutt. I don't think there'd been any chat-up lines.

'Keep your thing away from my Miriam. Just look at her! Traumatised she is. Traumatised! I might have to take her to the vet. Poor thing.'

Miriam, who had a much neater hairstyle than my own, appeared fine.

I managed to tighten my grip on the lead as Bossi licked his lips.

At least he's going after dogs rather than horses. But if this carries on, I'll have no arms left.

When we arrived home, I decided to make war with my hair. I shampooed it, rinsed it, combed it out with an Afro comb and repeated the trick. I checked the mirror.

Not too bad.

I returned to my bedroom and found a pair of blue trousers, a white shirt and a blue-and-white spotted tie on my bed.

'In case you're wondering what to wear!' shouted Maria from the hallway.

'Thank you!'

When I got dressed, I gazed into my wardrobe mirror and didn't mind the face staring back at me. 'Good to go,' I told it.

I made my way downstairs. I felt good.

Venetia and the crew are gonna be well shocked.

Maria paused from wiping the dinner table. She smiled and then stepped over to me.

'Didn't anyone teach you how to tie your own tie?' she asked.

'Er . . . no.'

She fixed my tie for me. 'There, that's better. Oh, and wear one of your blazers.'

'A blazer!' I protested.

'Yes, a blue one.'

'Have you been chatting to Mum?'

Maria smiled. 'I might have.'

A Crongton Christmas Party

I sighed before I climbed upstairs to fetch a royal blue blazer from my wardrobe.

'Now you look respectable.' Maria clapped. 'Don't forget to polish your shoes.'

I can't lie, even Bossi offered me a strange look of respect.

I made it to the church by 9.25 a.m.

Everyone was there, all neatly brushed up, suited and booted, apart from Juniper.

'If she doesn't come by nine-thirty, I'm stepping inside,' said Saira. 'Too cold to wait outside.'

'I'm with you on that.' Jonah nodded.

Just before it tick-tocked to 9.30 a.m., we spotted Juniper hot-stepping up the street. She wore a blue dress, a green floppy hat, a black bomber jacket and green Dr. Martens. Someone had styled her hair into plaits.

'I'm never late,' she said.

Also joining us was Liccle Bit's grandma, Granny Jackson. She wore this long, red coat and white shoes. Her white handbag was big enough for Liccle Bit to hide inside. As we entered the church, we heard the organ playing. Church folk were all polite smiles and friendly 'hellos'. We spotted Venetia in her black-and-red choir robes beyond the altar. We all waved at her. She half-smiled back at us. There were a lot of candles about the place. Granny Jackson made sure she sat next to McKay. The benches were hard.

'Good to see you, McKay,' Granny Jackson greeted. 'Merry Christmas to you all. Now, McKay, are you going to contribute to the Crongton soup kitchen's cake stall this year? Desmond and Clifton are looking for baking contributions. Church members are all cooking a liccle someting. They're serving Christmas dinners, puddings and cakes on Christmas Day at the community centre.'

McKay looked at me and then picked up the service pamphlet. 'Er . . . I'm not sure, Granny Jackson. It's a busy time.'

'Me sure it's a busy time for everyone,' Granny Jackson said. 'But the Lord will be most grateful if you can contribute. The carrot cake you made for Lemar's birthday was perfect. Not too dry like when so many others bake it. What do you say? Come on! Can't you find time to serve the Lord? If there is going to be a second coming, He will stop chasing the devil out of town and taste your cake first. Probably wid a scoop of raspberry ice cream.'

'Er . . . tings are about to boot off.'

The minister began the service. 'It's good to see so many new faces in church today as we celebrate the birth of Christ.'

He told the nativity story. He continued to preach that in our busy lives full of TV, devices and distractions, we should find a way to spend quality time with family and think about those who couldn't provide and be there for their children. I thought of Mum and Dad.

They need to hear this.

The choir sang the first three hymns. I spotted Venetia's folks sitting in the front pew, waiting for her moment.

'And now we have a solo sung by one of our choir members, Venetia,' introduced the minister.

Juniper got to her feet. So did Liccle Bit, McKay, Jonah and Saira. Granny Jackson pulled me up. The organ played. I felt nervous for my friend. Even the carved statue of an angel, high up on the wall, seemed to be listening. I glanced over my shoulder. The church was proper jammed. And Venetia sung her heart out to *God Rest Ye Merry, Gentlemen*.

'Yesssss!' hollered Liccle Bit. 'You blitzed it!'

'You blasted that carol into orbit!' yelled Saira.

'Crongton Knights forever!' shouted McKay. 'You mashed it!'

'Venetia! Beyoncé must bow to you!' Juniper cried out.

'Venetia!' I called out. 'You killed it! Crongton super-duper Knights!'

Everyone looked at us as the choir joined in for the second verse. I think the minister liked our energy.

Maybe not.

Even Granny Jackson was smiling and nodding. 'That was . . . beautiful,' she said. 'Just beautiful. Lemar, hold on to her good. Don't do anyting foolish.'

'I will, I will,' replied Liccle Bit.

We stepped out of church on a high. Granny Jackson said her goodbyes as we waited for Venetia.

'McKay. Don't forget,' Granny Jackson said. 'The Lord is waiting for your cake. Desmond and Clifton will be most grateful. If you can, drop it off in the morning so they can set up the pudding and cake table and make it look pretty.'

'I'll try and find the time,' replied McKay.

Five minutes later, Venetia rolled up. She was all big grins, bounce and high fives. She hugged everyone. 'Boy from the Hills!' She gazed at me. 'Is that you? Oh, my dumplings! Your hair. What did you do with it?'

'Er . . . just washed it,' I replied. 'That's all.'

'You look . . . you look.' Venetia tried to find words.

'Kinda human,' said Liccle Bit. 'Welcome to the brushed-up world.'

'Try and keep it like that for your party,' Saira said. 'No wilderness missions.'

Juniper pulled a face. 'But it's not you, is it?' she argued. 'Dressing up like that takes something away. Not gonna lie, I preferred the safari-gone-wrong look.'

'What's a safari-gone-wrong look?' I asked.

'When someone is running away from a peckish lion, and they have to escape through thick, prickly bushes with a mauled leg.'

'Oh,' I said.

'Not bad, not bad at all!' said another voice.

We all looked to our left. The Nicholas sisters. Venetia danced against them at the latest Crongton Games. I can't lie. They looked neat in their brown bear coats, red berets and white ankle boots.

'I give you ratings for your singing today, V,' said the taller one. 'It takes a trailer-load of guts to get up and sing to a Team Jesus audience.'

'Thanks,' said Venetia.

'My sistren can do anything when she puts her mind to it,' added Saira. 'Believe it, Alma.'

'She can do anything,' agreed Alma Nicholas. 'But she never beat us at the Crongton Games. We were robbed! We found out two of the judges live in South Crong.'

'Oh, boo bloody hoo!' mocked Liccle Bit. 'You lost fair and square, circle and triangle. Deal with it.'

'I don't care what anyone says,' said the younger sister. She stepped up close to Venetia, placed her hands on her hips and gave her the toe-to-forehead glare. 'We won that dance contest. Everyone knows it!'

'Tell her, Nikesha!' said Alma. 'There's a mural on a North Crong wall, near the basketball court, celebrating us beating your sad steps.'

'Liberties!' shouted Liccle Bit. 'Venetia and Saira won. Credits have rolled. The flowers were given out. End of!'

'We can settle this on Tuesday,' said Venetia.

'Where?' Alma asked.

'My man, Boy from the Hills, is having a fancy-dress rave at his gates this Tuesday evening,' revealed Saira. 'Come if you dare!'

Alma took another step closer to Venetia. Their noses were about an inch apart. They were like boxers at a weigh-in.

They're not gonna fight, are they?

'Do you think I'm scared of you?' said Alma. 'Anyplace, anytime, anywhere.'

'Bring it on,' added Nikesha.

'Reel back, reel back,' I said. 'Can't we have this dance-off somewhere else? I don't want anything to boot off at my place.'

'Boy from the Hills,' Saira replied. 'Stop fretting. When we finish with them, there will be blood on the dance floor. But it won't be ours.'

'No blood!' I said. 'No blood!'

The Nicholas sisters burst out laughing. 'You only won because of two crooked, bad-mind, corrupt South Crong judges.' Alma raised her voice. 'We're gonna stomp into your ends and show South Crong folk who really should have taken home the flowers from the Crongton Games.'

'Tell them!' added Nikesha.

'If I was you,' added Alma, 'I'd practise twenty-six hours a day! You're gonna need it.'

The Nicholas sisters linked arms and rolled away.

'They mean business,' I said.

'They can mean all the business they want,' said Liccle Bit. 'They're going down.'

'Can we step to the Crongton Party Exchange now?' asked McKay. He tapped his right foot on a lamp post.

'Black Panther, here I come!' said Jonah.

Liccle Bit pulled a face.

'I'll check on you guys later,' said Venetia. 'Saira and I got some new moves we have to learn.'

'We have?' asked Saira.

'I'll go with you,' said Juniper.

'Don't you need to get your outfit?' I asked.

Juniper grinned. Not sure what that meant.

11

The Crongton Party Exchange

The Crongton Party Exchange was on a side road off Crongton Broadway. Maple Avenue. It was in between a second-hand vinyl record shop and the Alabama Fried Chicken Hut. The front window display was full of Santas, elves, shepherds and Three Wise Men outfits. I had only been here once before when Mum bought me a Napoleon outfit for some French Revolution thing she hosted at my gates. After that night, I vowed to murder anyone with a mega-shovel who called me cute.

As Jonah and Liccle Bit hot-toed to the counter, I had a look around. There were King Kong masks, Godzilla costumes, Tinker Bell dresses, Peter Pan outfits, Tina Turner wigs, Harry Potter glasses, scarves and capes, Darth Vader helmets, wizard hats and even a Mahatma Gandhi wrap-around thing.

I hope it's clean.

In another corner were discounted Halloween masks and costumes of Frankenstein's monster, werewolves, Dracula and some ancient lady called Margaret Thatcher. *Who in the Crongton universe is she?*

Rubber skeletons hung from the ceiling. I couldn't quite tell if the cobwebs in the corners were fake or real. Michael Jackson's *Thriller* played on a low volume.

I made my way to the counter.

'What do you mean you have no more Black Panther costumes?' said Jonah. 'That's tragic. It's party season!'

'We had four in stock,' said the man behind the counter. He wore a T-shirt with a snake coming out of a skull's eye socket. He had tattoos of dragons and serpents all over his arms. He styled black nail polish. 'Last one went this morning.'

'You're not joking?' Jonah asked.

'Why would I be joking?' replied Tattoo Guy.

'That has deleted my party plans,' groaned Liccle Bit. 'What am I gonna do now?'

'Can't we interest you in anything else?' asked Tattoo Guy. 'Maybe Ant Man?'

Jonah and Liccle Bit swapped a glance before they checked around the store.

'Er . . . do you have any Robin Hood costumes?' I asked.

Tattoo Guy smiled. 'Yes, we most certainly do. Don't usually get requests for them until the spring.'

Ten minutes later, Liccle Bit had found a Bob Marley Rastafarian wig complete with denim trousers and jacket,

Jonah was more than happy he had discovered a Usain Bolt tracksuit and McKay settled on a Richard the Lionheart costume.

We stepped out of the shop. 'But Richard the Lionheart was white,' said Jonah.

'I know he was white,' replied McKay. 'But we're going to Boy from the Hills' Christmas rave. We're not filming a documentary.'

'Why Robin Hood?' Liccle Bit asked me.

'He lived in the woods, didn't he?' I replied. 'I live near woods. And my fave colour is green. And I wouldn't mind shooting arrows at Chapman and Thompson.'

'Would've been cool if they supplied bows and arrows with the costume,' said Liccle Bit.

'Wonder what the girls are coming as?' asked Jonah.

We said our goodbyes and I headed home.

12

Careless Whisper

To escape Maria's interrogation of the church service (she was Catholic), I decided to take Bossi for a walk. He was less energetic than usual. I wanted a change of scenery. I led him away from the woods along the Heath Road. We neared the Crongton Recreation Ground on the left before I made a left turn up Gravel Hill. The houses were proper expensive up here. Some properties had electric gates and high walls. I always loved the view offered at the top of the hill. You could see the whole forest, Crongton Heath, South Crong High and McKay and Liccle Bit's tower blocks. I could even make out the mud track where Wendy's dad trained his horses. My phone rang. It was Saira.

'My mum's fretting about your party,' she said.
'Oh? Why?'

'She thinks there's gonna be alcohol.'

'Alcohol!'

'Yeah, she wants to speak to your parents about it.'

'They're not here,' I replied.

'I didn't tell her that part.'

'I haven't told my parents about the party part either,' I confessed. 'They just think I'm having a couple of friends around to watch a movie on our big screen.'

'What am I going to do?' Saira asked. 'I *really* want to come. Especially as we're having a dance clash with the Nicholas sisters.'

'Make a clone of yourself in chemistry class, leave it in your room and the real you can step to my rave.'

'I'm serious!'

I thought about it.

'What are we gonna do?' Saira repeated. 'I can't let Venetia down.'

'Leave it with me,' I said. 'You said your mum wants to chat to my folks, right?'

'Yeah, she does.'

'And she's never spoken to or seen my folks before?'

'I don't think so,' Saira replied. 'I didn't see them at the last parents' evening.'

'OK, send me your mum's digits. Trust me, Saira, Cinderella will go to the ball.'

'Who's Cinderella?'

'Where you grew up, didn't your folks read to you any of *Grimm's Fairy Tales*?'

Careless Whisper

'Er . . . no. I remember my grandma reading me *Arabian Nights*.'

'Cool. Anyway, I think my plan might work.'

'Boy from the Hills. This is serious. What do you think the Nicholas sisters will say if I don't turn up? They'll spill to social media that I moused out. It'll be tragic. If my mum stops me from coming, I'll sneak out of my gates.'

'Let's not think about that.'

'I'm trusting you on this.'

'Yes, I know. Don't fret. Things are gonna roll sweetly.'

'Hmmmm. What is your plan?'

'OK, this is what I'm gonna do . . .'

13

Putting On the Ritz

Monday. One day before party time.

In the morning, I had browsed on the Internet searching for cool-looking water features to place in our garden. Wendy had texted me to say she was coming around 1 p.m. for our practice dance. I was home alone cos Maria had gone out shopping.

For lunch I had made a cheese, lettuce, Branston Pickle and ham sandwich. I had wedged a couple of slices of tomato in too. I was chasing it down with blackcurrant juice, when someone slapped the front door. I checked the time. 12.46 p.m.

It was Wendy. She looked good in her jeans, red Christmas reindeer jumper and white trainers. A green bangle niced up her left wrist. I thought about my dance lesson. Suddenly, my feet felt all strange.

'Are you ready?' she asked.

'Er . . . kind of. Just had my lunch.'

'You can dance it off,' she said.

'Not sure about that,' I replied. 'I'll probably break a leg.'

'Oh, ye of little confidence,' Wendy giggled.

I led her downstairs to the basement.

'I see you have cleared the dancing area,' Wendy said.

'Yeah, McKay helped me carry the pool table into the cinema room.'

'Great.' Wendy grinned. 'If you fall over, you won't hit your head on anything.'

'I'm not that bad,' I said.

'Hmmm.'

'What are we gonna dance to?' I asked.

'It's all on my phone.' Wendy smiled.

As Wendy fiddled with her mobile, I scratched my ear and took a few deep breaths.

Don't mess up! Don't mess up! Feet! Don't let me down.

Ariana Grande's *Just a Little Bit of Your Heart* tweeted out from Wendy's phone. My heartbeat felt like an angry King Kong pounding a small drum.

Be cool, be cool, be cool.

'Come here,' she said. 'Can't learn to dance with me if you're standing over there.'

'Er . . . no, I can't.'

I stepped over to Wendy. She smiled at me. She had nice brown eyes. 'Right,' she said. 'Put your arms around my neck.'

I did what I was told.

Never been this close to a girl before. Hope my nerves don't show.

'Relax your arms,' she instructed. 'Loosen up. You're not strangling my little brother – although he deserves it.'

'Oh, sorry.'

'OK, good. Now put one of your feet between mine,' she said. 'This will make sure that you *don't step on my toes*.'

'Which one? The left or the right?'

'Doesn't matter,' she replied.

I slid my right foot into place.

'OK, just rock gently from left to right,' she said. 'Don't move your feet too far, just half steps. Try to keep in time to the music.'

I followed Wendy's lead.

This is not too grubby. Not too difficult. It was kinda nice.

'You can move your chest a little closer to me,' she said. 'I did have a shower after I cleaned out the stables this morning.'

'Oh, sorry.'

'Mind you, my hair needs washing. I'll do it tomorrow morning before the party.'

For the next few minutes, no words were said. I felt comfortable. I dropped my hands and placed them on her waist. I sniffed Wendy's perfume, but I didn't have a clue what it was.

Do I need to slap on aftershave for my party? Have I got any aftershave? Better buy some.

The song finished. I didn't move until Wendy reached for her phone. 'You learn well,' she said. 'You're good for tomorrow. Just remember to keep relaxed. Don't move like a rusty robot.'

'Can you do me a big favour?' I asked. 'It's for a friend of mine.'

'What favour?'

'Pretend to be my mum.'

'Pretend to be your mum!' Wendy repeated. 'Not sure about that.'

'This friend at school. Her mum thinks I might be having alcohol at my gates tomorrow.'

'Alcohol?'

Wendy collapsed into giggles. She covered her mouth and almost fell over. As soon as she uncovered her mouth, she went into hysterics again.

'What's so funny?'

'I just . . . I just can't imagine you hosting a party with alcohol,' Wendy replied.

'I'm not hosting a party with alcohol!' I raised my voice. 'I'm just having a fancy-dress party.'

'Can't Maria do it?' Wendy asked.

'No. She's already keeping my rave a secret from my folks. And she's got a strong Filipino accent. It's gonna look well dodgy if she speaks to Saira's mum.'

'Saira?' Wendy asked. 'Do you fancy her?'

'No, she's just a friend. That's all.'

'You sure?'

'Of course I'm sure.'

'Is she pretty?' Wendy asked.

Gosh, how do I answer that without getting into trouble.

'Er . . . yes, Saira's pretty.'

'So, you *do* fancy her!'

'No, I don't,' I protested.

'Hmmm.'

I wanted to change the subject.

'Are you gonna do the favour or not?'

Wendy thought about it. She gave me a strange grin.

'OK. What do you want me to say?' Wendy asked.

'Er . . . just tell Saira's mum that you'll supervise the party, and no one will be allowed any drink. So, will you do it?'

Wendy side-eyed me.

'I do drama at school,' she said. 'Let's see if I can put it to use.'

'Triple thanks,' I said. 'I appreciate this to the max. One day, I'll go with you to one of your horse events.'

'Yeah, right.'

I punched in Saira's mum's number into my phone, placed it on speaker and passed it on to Wendy. She gave me a quick glance as the phone rang. She didn't look so confident.

'Yes, who is this?'

Immediately, I recognised Saira's mum's Syrian accent. Wendy sucked in a breath. She closed her eyes for a short second.

'This . . . this is Colin's mum, Mrs Scott,' Wendy said in a slightly deeper voice. 'I hope you don't mind me calling you like this, but I understand you have concerns about my Colin's party?'

'Thank you so much for calling,' Saira's mum replied. 'I appreciate that. Yes, I do have my concerns about the party.'

'What's worrying you?'

'First of all, will you and your husband be there to supervise everything? You know what kids are like these days. They're so impressionable. They're always . . . so fascinated with what they see on the Internet. You're not going out for the night, are you?'

'My husband has gone up to Scotland, but I'll be here,' said Wendy.

'Your husband has gone up to Scotland? What's he doing up there?'

'Er . . . um . . . he's campaigning about the lakes.'

I sensed Wendy losing her cool. She wiped her forehead.

Oh no, this could go wrong.

'Oh yes!' Saira's mum said. 'I watched something on the news the other day about it. They're pumping too much sewage into our lakes and rivers.'

'That's it! That's it!' Wendy raised her voice. 'He's campaigning about that.'

'I see. You live in a big house, Mrs Scott. Do you really think you can supervise so many teenagers with so many rooms?'

'Er . . .' Wendy replied. 'They must all remain in the basement where the party's being held. There's a toilet down there too. Snacks will be served from the kitchen.'

'That's good to know.'

'Don't worry, I'll make sure everyone behaves themselves,' Wendy said.

'I'm sure you will. I really appreciate you calling me. Maybe when you have time, you can come over to mine one day for a cup of tea and lunch. My place is not as big as yours, but it's comfortable. We make the best of it.'

'That would be lovely,' Wendy said.

I raised my hands and shook my head.

'That's very kind of you,' Wendy continued. 'I'll look forward to that.'

'I'll cook you something traditional,' Saira's mum said. 'Do you mind spices?'

'Love spices,' Wendy replied.

I gave Wendy a fierce side-eye.

'Bye then,' said Saira's mum. 'See you soon. Happy holidays.'

'Yes, goodbye. Nice to speak to you.'

Wendy killed the call. She turned to me and grinned.

'Are you cadazy?' I asked. 'How can you set up a meeting with Saira's mum?'

'She seems so nice,' replied Wendy. 'Wouldn't your mum want to meet her?'

'Probably yes, but she'll be meeting you. Oh, my daisies! Grasshoppers in a mash potato!'

Putting On the Ritz

'I could wear make-up to make me look older,' Wendy laughed. 'And dress up in your mum's clothes.'

'That's not gonna work.'

'Relax! Of course I'm not gonna meet up with her. I just said what I thought your mum might say. I reckon I done a good job. You should thank me for it.'

'Thanks,' I said. 'Really appreciate it. But no meetings with my friends' parents.'

'OK. Now that's out of the way. Let's do some more practice. We need to get rid of that robotic-ness out of your dancing.'

'Am I that bad?'

'Er . . . let's find a song.'

14

Jonah's Crush

An hour later, Maria arrived home. Wendy and I helped her carry the shopping into the kitchen.

'Jacket potato for lunch?' Maria offered. 'Got some tuna, chilli con carne, beans and cheese.'

'I've had lunch already, but I could fit in a jacket potato,' I said. 'Thanks very much.'

'Thank you, Maria,' Wendy said.

I was halfway through my jacket potato when someone smacked the letter box. I got up to see who was rattling the front door. Jonah. He looked like someone had chucked a bucket of stress over him.

'Thought I'd help you blow up your balloons and help with decorations,' he said.

'I was gonna do that in the morning,' I replied. 'What's up?'

Jonah's Crush

Jonah stared at the floor. 'The dirty truth is, my dad came around with Christmas presents and stuff and an argument booted off again. Tired of it. Thought I'd step around to yours and help you get ready for your rave.'

'What are they kicking off about?'

'Money,' replied Jonah. 'Always money. Mum wants more from Dad cos everything has gone up.'

'I guess we can start blowing up balloons this afternoon,' I said. 'Wendy's here. Maybe she can help too. Sorry to hear that your parents are warring again.'

'Now I think they should just get divorced and get it over and done with. Sick of it.'

Jonah followed me to the kitchen. Wendy was still enjoying her chilli con carne jacket potato and Maria was washing up stuff in the sink. She turned around and looked at Jonah.

'So, you're Jonah! Would you like a jacket potato? You can have a tuna, chilli-con-carne or baked-beans-and-cheese filling.'

Jonah stood there like he had been zapped into stillness by an alien with a ray gun. He struggled to get his mouth moving. Wendy giggled.

'Er . . . yes . . . um. Jacket potato,' Jonah stuttered. 'That would be excellent.'

'What do you want in it?' Maria asked again.

'Er . . . don't mind.'

'I'll give you tuna.'

Jonah managed to move his feet and take a seat at the dinner table. Wendy laughed some more.

'What's wrong with you?' I whispered to Jonah.

Jonah leaned towards me and spoke into my ear. 'You didn't tell me how pretty Maria is.'

'Jonah, she's twenty-two.'

'Will she be there at the party?'

'She's engaged,' I said.

'But will she be there at the party?' Jonah repeated.

'Yes, she's gonna help out McKay in the kitchen.'

Jonah pumped a fist. *'Yesssss!'*

'Did you hear what I said? She's engaged. Her fiancé works on cruise ships. And he's a lot bigger than you. Stop being a hound.'

'I'm not being a hound. I'm just appreciating a lady's beauty.'

'Start appreciating a lady your own age.'

Ten minutes later, Wendy said her goodbyes. Jonah and I started on the balloons.

'Maybe we can have one dance,' Jonah said. 'That won't hurt.'

'Jonah, listen to me keenly. You're fourteen. She's eight years older than you.'

'No problem,' Jonah replied. 'When I'm thirty-five, she'll be forty-three or so. No one will think twice about it.'

'It's not gonna work. Even if she *was* interested in you, she might get herself in trouble.'

'I'd never spill anything.'

'Isn't there any other girl who tickles your fancy?' I asked.

Jonah blew up a balloon as he thought about it.

Jonah's Crush

I decided to take Bossi for an early walk and then get back to the decorations.

'Bossi! Bossi!'

We heard his paws stomping down the stairs. He must've been asleep on my bed.

Jonah paused from tying up a balloon and turned to me. 'In the name of Godzilla, what is that?'

Before I could answer, Bossi pawed into the basement, wagged his tail and stood on his hind legs.

Oh my daisies, he's tall.

Jonah's eyes did this horror movie victim thing before he hot-toed up the stairs. 'Don't let it near me!'

'He's harmless,' I said.

'That thing doesn't look harmless!'

Jonah disappeared.

I found him in the kitchen. He sat on a stool beside Maria. He gazed at her as if she was a Bond girl. 'You shouldn't have to work with a man-eater,' he said to her. 'You should ask extra for danger money.'

I found Bossi's lead and secured it to his neck. He was still a bit excited.

'I should ask extra for everything else.' Maria nodded.

'What is that thing?' Jonah asked.

'A dog,' I replied. 'He's tame.'

'It hasn't monster-munched anyone? You might have a Jurassic Park tragedy if that thing is let loose in the party.'

Maria giggled.

'He'll be tied up in the garden on a long lead,' I said. 'Why don't you come on our walk and get to know him?'

Jonah stared at Bossi, then glanced at Maria. He half-smiled at her. 'Er ... yeah, I can do that,' he said. 'Mega-dogs don't scare me.'

'We'll finish the balloons when we get back,' I said.

'OK.' Jonah nodded. 'But if I go missing, you're gonna have to look inside that dinosaur and see if I'm in there.'

'Like Jonah in the whale,' chuckled Maria.

Jonah didn't laugh.

We headed outside. Jonah walked ten metres behind me.

15

A Tight Fit

Tuesday morning. The day of the party.

My conscience told me to ring Dad or Mum and tell them about the rave. But no.

It's too late for that. They might wanna talk me out of it. It'll be a nightmare on Crongton Heath if I try to turn people away in fancy dress when they arrive at my gates.

They decided to jet up to Scotland to rage about grimy lakes on *Christmas week*. I can't lie, I felt a dose of nerves.

Say they come back early?

It was 9.15 a.m. when my phone rang. It was DJ Teaspoon.

'Have you ordered the ride yet?' he asked. 'Crongton's number one DJ has to get set.'

'You mean order the taxi?'

'Yes, yes, the ride. Have you ordered it yet?'

'Er . . . no. Just got up.'

A Crongton Christmas Party

'You *just got up*,' DJ Teaspoon repeated. 'I've gotta get my stuff to your mansion and test it out, make sure everything's on point.'

'OK, OK,' I said. 'What time do you want me to hook you?'

'Hook me at ten-thirty.'

'Ten-thirty! That leaves me only an hour and a bit. First I have to take Bossi for a walk.'

'OK, let's say eleven. Eleven-fifteen at the latest. But don't be late, a long wait this DJ won't appreciate. Set your sat navs to my gate. Don't get robbed by the South Crong kerb hustlers, for goodness' sake.'

'You're gonna rap too?' I asked.

'If the vibes are good,' he said. 'By the way, my apprentice DJ, Mellow Enchanter, can't make it. You don't have to worry about sending a cab for her. Her fam have gone to her granny's place in Elmers End for Christmas.'

'Oh.'

'But it's all still good.'

'I don't know your address.'

DJ Teaspoon texted me his details.

Bossi had slept in the basement. I can't lie, the balloons and bunting gave the place a happy vibe. I couldn't remember a childhood birthday party. I probably didn't have enough friends back then. Sleepovers were something other kids did. I closed my eyes and imagined everyone dancing and bubbling in their fancy dress.

I arrived at DJ Teaspoon's place just after half-eleven. He

A Tight Fit

lived on a nice road off the Crongton Circular between South and North Crong. His front garden could have done with a little work, but the back lawn was neat and tidy with a small tree in the middle. As he loaded the taxi with his Bluetooth speakers, laptop, headphones and wires, McKay called.

'Are you coming to get me?' McKay asked.

'I'm just picking up DJ Teaspoon.'

'I need to carry my blender and my other utensils to your castle,' McKay said. 'And they will get heavy on the trod to your ends.'

'All right, we'll pick you up on the way back to my place.'

The taxi driver tapped his fingers on the steering wheel as we waited outside McKay's slab.

How much is this gonna cost me?

'Glad that everyone's getting into the fancy dress vibe,' I said. 'People are taking it serious.'

'Why not?' said DJ Teaspoon. 'When do South Crong school peeps get the chance to dress up and go to a rave?'

McKay climbed into the back seat as I moved into the front. It was a bit of a squeeze. I spotted all kinds of seasonings in his bag, and his treasured blenders. Once I asked to borrow one of them, but he said, wherever his blender goes, he follows.

'DJ Teaspoon,' McKay greeted him. 'Make sure you play some Afrobeats and reggae.'

'I play a little bit of everything,' DJ Teaspoon replied. 'I go with the flow, musical tastes for any Sam or Joe, after this gig, just watch my rep grow.'

A Crongton Christmas Party

'Just remember, you're playing to a South Crong crowd,' McKay said. 'They don't wanna hear too much pop or country.'

'Not even Beyoncé?' DJ Teaspoon replied.

'Not even Beyoncé,' McKay repeated. 'Her last album went all a bit yee-hah.'

'It sold well,' argued DJ Teaspoon. 'Might play one or two tracks off it.'

'If you get a bad response then don't be surprised.'

'I know what I'm doing,' said DJ Teaspoon. 'Do I tell you how to cook your mince pies or chicken patties? No. So, don't be telling me about my business.'

'I'm trying to help your business,' argued McKay. 'A South Crong crowd is hard to please. They flung paper cups at the DJ at the last community centre rave.'

'Rewind, rewind!' I said. 'I don't want anything booting off in the car. You're both very important to my rave. And you're both top of the ratings in what you do.'

DJ Teaspoon and McKay side-eyed each other. I didn't think their feud was over.

Ten minutes later, we arrived at my gates. I helped DJ Teaspoon carry his stuff to the basement. On the way back to the taxi to pick up the wires, I thought I spotted someone near the entrance of my driveway.

I checked the road that led to my gates and looked across the Heath. Didn't see anyone. I peered into the woods. No movement. I stood still for a minute or so, listening. Nothing. Only the winter breeze passing through the bony branches.

A Tight Fit

I returned to my house. I gave DJ Teaspoon a small table to work on. He placed his speakers in two corners of the room.

'Did you see anyone near my gates when the taxi pulled up?' I asked DJ Teaspoon.

'No,' he replied. 'Your mansion is proper remote. Didn't see anyone.'

'Are you *sure*?'

'Why you asking?'

'Thought I scoped Vincent Chapman at the top of my driveway.'

'Vincent Chapman!' DJ Teaspoon laughed. 'You're getting paranoid, Boy from the Hills. Your place is hard to find even for a sat nav. With Chapman's brain, how's he gonna find it? Relax. Chapman and Thompson are probably hanging outside a sweet shop jacking some poor Year Seven kid's pocket money.'

'Someone spilled,' I said. 'Even the Nicholas sisters knew about my rave. They're having a dance-off with Saira and Venetia.'

'That's gonna be the bomb,' replied DJ Teaspoon. 'I'm going to record that and slap it on my YouTube channel. And don't fret about Chapman and Thompson. Even if they did know your address, they'll get lost in the Crongton wilderness.'

'I hope you're right.'

'I am right. OK, I need a mug of coffee to get my DJ day booting.'

I went to the kitchen to check in on McKay. DJ Teaspoon followed me. He switched the kettle on and made his coffee.

McKay had his white chef's hat, his mum's apron and a pair of surgical gloves on. He hummed along to a song chirping out from his phone.

'Did you see any folks hanging about the top of my driveway when we arrived at my gates?'

'Nope,' replied McKay. 'But I wasn't really looking out the window. I was making sure DJ Teaspoon didn't crush my utensils bag with his big feet. It was a tight fit in there.'

'Can I help?' I asked.

'Yeah,' he said. 'You can knead the pastry for the chicken rolls when it's ready. Wash your hands and pull on a pair of gloves.'

I wasn't really a kitchen person, but I really enjoyed helping McKay with the baking. He whistled as he worked, sometimes singing along to whatever tune played from his phone. At the back of my mind, I couldn't help but wonder if it really was Chapman I spotted near my gates.

Maybe my mind is beginning to play tricks on me. Boy from the Hills, relax. It's gonna be a good day.

Just after we put in the first tray of chicken rolls, we heard DJ Teaspoon test out his Bluetooth speakers.

'It's I, DJ Teaspoon at the party control, come to make the good times roll, I come with no virus, I come with no trolls, everyone having a bubbling time, that's my goal.'

I went downstairs. The bassline boomed from the twin speakers. DJ Teaspoon held a headphone to his left ear

A Tight Fit

while concentrating on his playlist on his laptop screen. He bopped his head.

'Sounds good to me!' I shouted. 'Are you gonna wear a costume?'

'I've got a cape,' he replied.

'You're coming as Batman? Superman?'

'No, Musicman,' he laughed. 'Why can't DJ folks get to fly and save the world.'

'How?' I wondered.

'By playing a particular tune that drives the villain away.'

'O . . . K.'

'Colin!' Maria called from upstairs. 'Someone at the door. Last time I looked, I'm not your doorman.'

'Back in a sec,' I said to DJ Teaspoon.

Someone's early. It's just gone three o'clock.

I opened the front door. It was Merlene Quarrie, Saira's plus one. She looked magnificent in a gold-spangled dress, red high heels and a beehive wig that nearly kissed the ceiling. Her cherry-coloured lipstick nearly blinded me.

'Wow!'

Merlene smiled.

'Er . . . let me guess . . . Jennifer Hudson?'

'No.'

'Whitney Houston.'

'No.'

'Rihanna.'

'Nope. Can't you guess?'

I shook my head.

'I'm Diana Ross from the Supremes.'

'Who? The Supremes? Never heard of them.'

'You know back in the day. Motown.'

'Motown?' I repeated.

'You need a course in the history of soul music.'

'Can't know everything,' I said. 'Anyway, thanks for coming and dressing up. You look ace.'

'No worries . . . Listen, can we talk somewhere private?'

'Er, about what?'

Merlene whispered into my ear. 'About me and Saira.'

'You wanna talk to *me* about that?'

'Yeah, why not.'

'Me?'

'Yes, you.'

'OK, follow me.'

I led her to one of the guest bedrooms upstairs. 'What a long hallway you have!' Merlene said. 'In the winter months, I could do my running training here.'

I laughed. We passed Maria on the way. She gave me a funny look.

Don't know why Maria might think that Merlene's in any danger from me. Mind you, Wendy might not love *the thought I'm up here with another girl. I wonder what time she'll arrive?*

Maria must've cleaned the room recently. I sniffed the lavender air freshener. The wide window offered a neat view of our back garden.

I sat down at the dressing table. Merlene parked on the

A Tight Fit

bed. There was a framed picture of L. S. Lowry's *Coming from the Mill* hanging over the bed headboard. Liccle Bit told me L. S. Lowry was an old-school top-ranking artist.

'How can I help?' I asked.

'I just wanna get your opinion and what you think others might say.'

'About what?'

'Me and Saira . . . We're getting quite close. Not a lot of folks know that. You won't freak out if you see us dancing with each other?'

'Freak out?' I repeated. I chuckled. 'The whole crowd will probably freak if they see me dance!'

'No, seriously. What do you think?'

'For me, it's not breaking news. You're dancing with Saira. So what?'

'Do you think peeps will chat?'

'Merlene, if there is one thing that I've learned about attending South Crong High, folks chat about anyone and everything.'

'That's true.'

'You really like her, don't you,' I said.

Merlene thought about it for a couple of seconds. She nodded.

'She's been through a lot,' I added. 'You know, the stuff with her dad. Being in one of them refugee places.'

'Yeah, I know,' Merlene replied. 'Don't worry, I don't wanna hurt her. We're taking it slow, you know, getting to know each other.'

'If you really like her,' I said, 'then why should you care what folks think?'

'Yeah, you're right.' Merlene nodded. 'Why should I care? Look how many school peeps are coming out as gay.'

'Exactly. It's not a biggie any more.'

'In some communities it is,' replied Merlene.

'Colin!' Maria called from the upstairs hallway. 'Someone at the door.'

'I thought peeps would come about five or six. It's just after three.'

'That's a good sign,' said Merlene.

Merlene followed me downstairs. I opened the front door. Jonah wore a puffa jacket. He pulled it off to reveal his Usain Bolt tracksuit and Jamaican running vest. He rocked a pair of yellow, green and black trainers. I wondered if the footwear was a Christmas present from his dad.

He did the Usain Bolt archery pose. He remained in that position for a long second. I guessed he wanted to impress Maria. Merlene clapped as Maria smiled.

'The most rapid *man* in the world has reached,' Jonah said. 'Is the beast tied up in the garden?'

'Yes,' I replied. 'Didn't think folks would start coming so early.'

'This is Crongton,' Jonah said. 'If you want food at a party, you have to get there early.'

Merlene laughed and nodded.

Jonah pulled out an envelope from his manbag for Maria. 'This is for you,' he said.

A Tight Fit

He handed it to her. It was a Christmas card with an image of an angel. 'How sweet,' Maria said. 'That's very kind of you. A merry Christmas to you too. I'll put it on my bedside cabinet.'

Jonah grinned like he had just won a gold medal. 'Can I help with the cooking?' he called out as he stepped towards the kitchen.

'We're good,' said McKay. 'Come back when there's washing-up to be done.'

'Boy from the Hills,' Jonah called. 'Aren't you gonna dress up in your costume?'

'Yeah,' I said. 'Listen out for the door. Don't let any clowns in. Especially the ones with the white powdered faces.'

'What's with you and clowns?' replied Jonah.

'It's a long story.'

Once upon a time, I watched this horror series called *IT*. It gave me nightmares for the longest time. Don't like to think about it.

I went upstairs and changed into my Robin Hood outfit. I checked myself in the mirror. I didn't look too bad. The green hat with a brown feather sticking out of it was a perfect fit. Not as glamorous as Merlene, but Wendy might appreciate it.

By the time I got downstairs, Saira had arrived. She had these baggy cream-coloured trousers on. She rocked white platform trainers. Around her waist, she wore a wide red silk belt tied up in a bow. She styled a beige-coloured shirt and a purple waistcoat. Jonah and Merlene admired her costume as I tried to figure out who she was.

'Aladdin!' Merlene said. 'You look fabuloscious. Only thing missing is the lamp.'

'I tried to find one in Crong market,' replied Saira. 'No luck.'

'How are you supposed to dance with that thing anyway,' said Merlene.

'And Boy from the Hills!' Saira turned to me. 'You look green-o-liscious.'

'Robin Hood definitely suits you,' added Jonah. 'Where's Venetia and Liccle Bit?'

'Oh, they'll be along later,' Saira replied. She turned to Merlene. 'Looking glam, girl.'

'And you're looking all pantomimey.'

'I do my best,' said Saira. She sniffed something. 'What's cooking?'

We all smelt the aroma drifting over from the kitchen. My tastebuds wanted to come out and play.

'When's food served?' called out Jonah.

'Five-thirty on the dot,' replied McKay. 'Chicken rolls, mince pies and patties. No D-rate school dinner crap.'

'Can't we have a sample now?' Jonah asked.

'Most definitely not!' replied McKay. 'Be gone from my kitchen!'

16

Mrs Smythe-Watson

I licked my lips as the front door rapped again. I don't know why, but I expected it to be Wendy.

It wasn't her. Standing in front of me was one of my neighbours. Mrs Smythe-Watson. She lived about seventy metres away in a stone house that had little balconies jutting out from the upstairs windows. In the summer months, sometimes I spotted her with a pair of binoculars peering towards the Heath. She was always shouting at her gardener, Mr Everton Bennett, who had given me tips over the years. Her husband built this humongous man cave in their back garden where he had a snooker table and a cinema screen. He even had a bed in there.

Before she spoke, she ran her eyes over my outfit. 'Merry Christmas, young Colin.'

'Merry Christmas, Mrs Smythe-Watson.'

A Crongton Christmas Party

'What is that awful booming sound?'

'Oh, just the music.'

'You call that music? Sounds like earthquakes erupting from your basement. I can hear it from my front garden.'

I closed the door behind me.

She was dressed in brown knee-length boots, a light-blue coloured raincoat, a dark-blue scarf and a beige and light-brown checked deerstalker hat.

'Is everything in order?' she asked.

'Yeah,' I replied. 'Just having a few friends around.'

'I've seen all manner of kids dressed up in heaven knows what enter your home.'

'Yeah, I'm having a fancy-dress party. Anything wrong in that?'

'If you were hosting a fancy-dress party, your parents would have informed me.'

'They're not here.'

'Oh . . . I see. Hmmm. If I was informed, I would have baked you a cake.'

'Maria's here,' I added. 'In case you're worried about anything.'

'And most of your friends attend South Crongton High?'

'Er . . . yeah,' I replied. 'What's wrong with that? That's where I go to school.'

'Yes . . . Quite. *All* the same, perhaps I might drop by later on and check that everything's in order.'

'That's not necessary,' I said.

Mrs Smythe-Watson

'Kids get up to anything these days, young Colin. You can't have eyes in the back of your head.'

Suddenly, I heard Bossi barking from the back garden.

'Er, excuse me, Mrs Smythe-Watson,' I said. 'Just gonna check on Bossi.'

'You have a dog?'

'It's not mine. I'm looking after it.'

Mrs Smythe-Watson shook her head.

I went through the side door to reach my garden. Bossi had stepped to the far side of the garden near the back wall. I hoped he wouldn't stomp all over my rosemary bush. I checked his lead was still secure around his neck. He yapped at something. His eyes were alert. His legs were ready to pounce.

'What are you making your noise at?' I asked him. He stopped barking, stood on his hind legs and licked my face with his long tongue.

I stopped to listen and peered over the wall. I couldn't hear or see anything. Maybe Bossi's still getting used to my place. I stroked his back to reassure him.

'Are you hungry? I'll get Maria to cook you your duck or rabbit meat. Sorry I have to leave you outside.'

I was about to go back inside via the back door, but remembered I had left Mrs Smythe-Watson outside at the front.

'Whose dog is it?' she asked.

'Mrs Utili,' I replied.

'Mrs Utili,' she repeated. 'Off on her holidays again, is

she? She's hardly been at home since her dear husband passed. Sweet man he was. He loved his walks in the Crongton Hills.'

'He loved his whisky too.'

'Colin! Don't speak ill of the dead.'

'Can I get back to my guests now? I have to take their coats upstairs and show them where everything is.'

'OK, then. I'll drop by later to see how you're getting on. Hosting a party can be hard work. And someone *always* misbehaves.'

'Merry Christmas, Mrs Smythe-Watson.'

'Merry Christmas, young Colin.'

17

A Holy Presence

Mrs Smythe-Watson turned and made her departure. I breathed out a sigh of relief before I went back inside. Jonah helped Maria dry up a few dishes. It was kinda strange imagining Usain Bolt doing his chores.

I went downstairs and Merlene and Saira were already dancing.

This is gonna be all good. Folks are enjoying themselves.
Rat-a-tat-tat!
Am I gonna spend more time at my front door than the party? I hope it's not Mrs Smythe-Watson again.

It wasn't. Maria, McKay and Jonah joined me to take a closer look. It was Jesus Christ, complete with ankle-length white robes, sandals and a long blonde wig. He wasn't wearing any socks. A wooden cross dangled from a silver chain around his neck. I glanced at Jonah, and he looked horrified. Jesus stood there with who I thought was Tina Turner. She rocked high-heeled leather boots, some kind of black corset thing and a huge spiky blonde wig. I think I was in shock for a few seconds as I took their coats.

'Kiran?' McKay managed. 'Kiran Cassidy?'

'Yep, it's me. Is there a prize for this fancy-dress thing?'

'Maybe an extra chicken pattie,' replied McKay. 'Not getting that till five-thirty, though.'

'And Tina Turner.' Jonah pointed at Caroline Stringer. 'It's gonna look well strange, you two bubbling together.'

Kiran did a little dance move. Even in a Jesus robe, he could move very well. I wondered what Mrs Smythe-Watson would have made of it. She'd probably get all biblical and stone the both of them.

Maria just smiled. 'At least we now have someone to say grace before we eat,' she said.

'What's cooking?' Kiran asked. 'If you're making fifty mince pies, maybe I can turn them into a thousand.'

'Can I have a sample?' asked Caroline.

'Um . . . OK.' McKay nodded. 'You can have one mince pie each but nothing else until five-thirty. I don't wanna run out too early.'

'And I'm thirsty, man,' moaned Kiran.

Maria poured lemonade, Coke Zero and orangeade into paper cups. She placed them on a tray and offered them to guests.

'I could've done that for you,' said Jonah.

A Holy Presence

I took the coats and placed them in Dad's office, then returned for my mince pie. Even I wasn't allowed more than one.

The mince pie was good. Nice and hot. The pastry was on point. I licked my fingers when my letter box was slapped again. I opened the front door.

Oh my gosh.

It was Ava Cohen. She took off her coat and gave it to me. She styled a red corset thing with a gold tiara crowning her long black hair. She wore spangly three-quarter trousers and knee-length black boots.

'Wonder Woman's here,' I said.

McKay was the first to acknowledge Ava. He dropped his wooden spoon and made his way to the front door. He blessed his eyes on her for a long second before he spoke. 'Oh, my omelettes!' he said. 'You . . . you came!'

'You invited me,' Ava replied. 'I thought, not doing anything so dramatic over the holiday, so let me step to Boy from the Hills' party.'

'Thank you soooo much for coming, Ava,' said McKay. 'In fact, your timing's perfect. I've just taken the first stash of mince pies out of the oven. Do you wanna sample one? Maybe two?'

'This is not a Christmas celebration, is it? Mince pies? Elves, turkeys, Santas, Christmas carols?'

'No, no, not at all, 'McKay said. 'It's just a normal fancy-dress party. No celebrating of baby Jesus here.'

A Crongton Christmas Party

Just then, Jesus Christ, or as I knew him, Kiran Cassidy, stepped towards the front door. He munched a mince pie and sank a paper cup full of Coke Zero. The wooden cross he rocked looked twice as big as when I first saw it. Pure panic spread over McKay's face. I thought he was gonna have a stroke or something.

'This is not what it looks like,' McKay said. 'There will be no breaking of bread, no turning water into wine, no donkeys in a stable, no shepherds and Jesus will not be conducting the choir for Christmas carols.'

Ava burst out laughing.

Kiran nodded at Ava. 'What's good, Ava. You wanna sample these mince pies? They're all delish – McKay does have his uses.'

'So . . . so you're OK with Kiran dressing up as Jesus?' McKay asked Ava.

'Of course I am.' Ava smiled. 'It's a fancy-dress party, right. I was just winding you up.'

Ava looked at me. 'And a big hello to you, Robin Hood. You are Robin Hood, right? Not one of those eco folks who stop traffic on the Crong circular?'

'I'm Robin Hood.' I nodded. 'Thank you for making it to my rave.'

'You have a beautiful house,' complimented Ava. 'I hope you don't mind but I invited my friend Shira. She'll be along later. Hope that's OK.'

'No, we don't mind,' said McKay. 'Do we?'

McKay side-eyed me and nodded.

A Holy Presence

'No probs,' I said. 'She's welcome.' I pointed the way to the kitchen. 'Get yourself a mince pie and a drink. I think McKay might give you two.'

McKay served Ava with two mince pies and then asked me if he could go up to my room and change into his costume.

'Why can't *I* have two mince pies?' I wondered. 'It's my party and I should be able to munch when I want to.'

'Cos if I give you two, everyone will want two. Stop grumping.'

'Stop grumping!' I repeated. '*I* bought the mince pies. It's *my* kitchen.'

'Yes, you bought the mince pies and everything else,' said McKay. 'But are you as pretty as Ava? Hell, no!'

'That's cold,' I said.

'Cold, but the dirty truth.'

McKay went upstairs. I stole an extra mince pie. Three bites. Lovely.

Someone slapped the front door. I wiped the crumbs from my lips and went to answer it. It was Liccle Bit, Venetia and Juniper. Liccle Bit was dressed up as a mini Bob Marley. He sang *Three Little Birds* as he entered.

'We've had to listen to that all along the way here,' said Juniper.

Juniper had green paint all over her face and hands. She wore a bright red lipstick and long eyelashes. Her witch's hat was tall and made from black felt. Her black cloak reached down to her knees. Her false nails were so long she could've fought a sword fight with the Three Musketeers. She wore black lace-up boots. If there was gonna be a fancy-dress contest, the winner had to be her. She even had a snarl going on. She looked more like the Wicked Witch of the West in the *Wizard of Oz* movie than the actress who played her.

'I think you've messed up your chance with Kiran Cassidy,' I laughed.

'Is he here? Why?'

'He's dressed up as Jesus Christ.' I grinned. 'Can't see Jesus dancing with a witch. That's just all wrong.'

'He will,' insisted Juniper. 'Trust me, he will, my pretty!'

'Kiran's with Caroline Stringer,' Jonah said.

'Or Tina Turner,' I cut in.

'You're gonna have to deal with it,' added Venetia. She was dressed all in white like a tennis player, complete with skirt, white socks, name-brand top and headband. I guessed she came as Coco Gauff.

Juniper smiled. 'Tina Turner? Hmmm. Nobody will hear her sing or scream in the woods. It's gonna be a long night, my pretty.'

'Everyone looks great,' said Venetia. She looked towards the kitchen. 'Where's McKay?'

'Getting changed,' I replied. 'You can munch one mince pie now and more later.'

Everyone collected their mince pies and drinks from the kitchen and then went downstairs.

A Holy Presence

I started to wonder when Wendy would arrive.

Why would she teach me to dance if she wasn't gonna come? Maybe she doesn't like me as much as I thought? Perhaps she just wants me to stay stuck in the friend zone? I checked my phone. *Nearly 4 p.m. Shall I call her? No. Too needy. It's still early. Give her time.*

DJ Teaspoon rocked the basement. Maria had kept him supplied with mugs of coffee. He had everyone bubbling. Jesus Christ performed the moonwalk. Even I bust a few moves. They weren't great but I think I was better than Dad at our last New Year's Eve party (he was a bit drunk). McKay joined us in his Richard the Lionheart costume. He even wore a rusty gold crown. Everyone loved it.

Man! Hosting a party was the best idea I ever had.

I was dancing with Liccle Bit and Jonah when I spotted someone coming down the stairs. It was Wendy. Relief flowed through me. I couldn't remember the jockey's name who she came as, but she looked fabuloscious.

OK, OK, Colin. Don't say anything weird. Be cool. Try not to make it obvious how pretty she is.

'You look mega awesome,' I said to her. 'Who have you come as again?'

Wendy slapped me gently on the forehead. 'Rachael Blackmore!'

'Oh, yes,' I remembered. 'Winner of the Big National.'

'The Grand National!' she corrected

'Welcome to my Christmas rave,' I said. 'As you can see, everyone is fizzing.'

Wendy ran her eyes over the guests. 'They sure are,' she agreed. 'So much energy. You'll have to introduce me to your friends. I only know McKay and Jonah.'

Before I could introduce Wendy to anyone else, Saira bounced up to us. 'Is this Wendy?' she asked me.

'Yep, this is Wendy, master of horses.'

'Thanks so much for speaking to my mum,' Saira said. 'She totally thought it was Boy from the Hills' mum. Really appreciate it. Feel a bit guilty now it's done, but what else could I do? I didn't want to miss this party.'

'Glad I could help out,' Wendy replied. 'Great costume. Aladdin, right?'

'Yep, Aladdin.'

'By the way,' I cut in. 'Who let you in?'

'Maria. She said you were dancing.'

'If you can call it that,' I laughed.

'Come on, Colin,' Wendy urged. 'Let's start bubbling.'

For the next half an hour, I wasn't sure what I was doing with my feet or the moves I tried to make with them. But no one cared. DJ Teaspoon played some walloping tunes. Everyone was having their best party time. Hands were up in the air like they just didn't care. Whenever the crowd liked a tune, they hollered *'rewind'*. DJ Teaspoon did his thing while bopping his head this way and that.

'Who comes from the east side?' he asked the crowd.

'BOOOOOO!'

'Who comes from the west side?'

'BOOOOOO!'

A Holy Presence

'Who comes from the north side?'
'BOOOOOO! BOOOOOO! BOOOOOO!'
'Who comes from the south side?'
'YAYYYYYYYYYY!'

18

The Nicholas Sisters vs Saira and Venetia

I had worked up a sweat when Maria came down the stairs and called me. 'Someone at the door. My hands are greasy. I'm going to wash up then feed Bossi. His duck meat is ready.'

I went upstairs to answer the front door. Two girls dressed in black morning suits, bow ties and top hats stood in front of me. The Nicholas sisters. Silver glitter blessed their cheeks. Alma was slightly taller than Nikesha. I can't lie. They looked magnificent, complete with their black shiny tap-dancing shoes.

'Is this your house?' Alma asked me.

'Of course it is,' I replied. 'Why wouldn't it be?'

'And you go to South Crong High?' asked Nikesha.

'Yep, I sure do.'

The girls swapped a look.

'As promised, we're here,' said Alma. 'Bus from North Crong isn't cheap. We're laying down the challenge.'

'We're prepped and dancehall ready,' added Nikesha. 'Where's our weak competition?'

'Downstairs,' I replied. 'Do . . . do you want a mince pie and a soft drink before you go down?'

They exchanged another look.

'That's the first piece of niceness I have ever experienced standing on South Crong turf,' said Alma.

'You're not lying,' added Nikesha.

'Yes, we'll sample a mince pie and a drink.' Alma nodded. 'Thank you. Are you sure you attend South Crong High?'

'I'm proper sure,' I said.

'But you can't really call yourself a South Crongtonian,' Nikesha said. 'You live out here on Crong Heath. This is neutral lands where the long-boot and fox-chaser peeps live.'

'I'm South Crong to my bone marrow,' I said.

I led them to the kitchen and served them a mince pie each. They chased it down with Coke Zero.

Alma looked at Nikesha. She licked her lips. 'Are you ready, sis?'

'Been ready since I was born,' Nikesha replied.

'Let's do this!'

'OK,' I said. 'I wanna see some electric boogie-loogie moves on the dance floor. No blood.'

'Electric boogie-loogie?' Alma laughed. 'What century are you in?'

They followed me downstairs. Everyone stopped dancing.

Even DJ Teaspoon did a double take. He spoke into the microphone.

'Crowd of people, all the way from North Crong, to lay down their challenge to Saira and Venetia, are the Nicholas sisters. It's gonna be brutal. Survival of the fittest. Blood will be rippling on the dance floor. Only two can survive. It's the mother of all dance clashes. Everyone start recording. This is gonna go viral. Aliens will be watching this on their devices on Mars. Galaxies we've never heard of will be tuning in.'

I joined Wendy.

'Gosh! This is so exciting,' she said. 'Never seen a live dance contest.'

'This is no *Strictly*,' I said.

'That's what makes it so cool,' Wendy replied.

Saira and Venetia approached the Nicholas sisters. 'We accept your challenge,' Venetia said. 'We respect that you stepped all the way from North Crong for this dance-off, but you're going back with no flowers and no medals.'

Nikesha stepped forward. She glared at Saira and Venetia. I sensed the tension in the room. DJ Teaspoon dropped the volume. Nobody could pull their eyes away from the dancers.

'The Nicholas sisters look totally awesome in their morning suits,' Wendy whispered into my ear.

'You're not wrong,' I agreed. 'Venetia and Saira gonna have to be on top of their game.'

'As we've come from North Crong,' said Nikesha. 'We get to select the music we dance to.'

The Nicholas Sisters vs Saira and Venetia

Venetia and Saira thought about it.

'What's a matter?' said Alma. 'Feeling nervous? You're about to get mashed in your own backyard? I'd feel proper anxious too.'

'Don't bother us,' replied Saira. 'Select whatever tune you like. You better add something they play at funerals too. You might need it.'

Alma stepped over to DJ Teaspoon. She whispered something into his ear as he sipped his coffee. DJ Teaspoon tapped a few keys on his keyboard. Jesus Christ picked up a chair from the cinema room, stood on it, and began recording on his phone.

Juniper raised a fist. *'South Crong forever!'*

I spotted Maria watching from the stairs. Liccle Bit said a quick prayer.

When did he turn religious?

Merlene went over to Saira, gave her a quick hug and held her hands. 'I know how good you are,' she said. 'You proper got this!'

The Nicholas sisters did their stretch exercises. DJ Teaspoon performed his beatboxing skills on the mic. McKay munched another mince pie. I should've asked him to make some popcorn.

'Who goes first?' DJ Teaspoon asked.

'Let Aladdin and Tennis Barbie go first,' said Alma.

'Makes no difference to us,' said Saira. 'The penguins can try to follow if they're brave enough.'

The crowd formed a circle. Saira and Venetia stepped

inside it. They sucked in long breaths. They flexed their legs and stretched their backs. Juniper stood on a table.

'DJ!' Venetia shouted. 'Roll that tune!'

A solid bassline blitzed the room. Venetia and Saira began their routine. Their movements were timed to perfection. Every step, twist and head movement was a joy to watch. They did flips, slides and kicks. Everyone raised their hands in the air. Whistles were blown. Adrenaline hot-flashed through my veins. Liccle Bit started a chant.

> *'Go, South Crong!*
> *Go, South Crong!*
> *Go, South Crong!'*

Even Wendy joined in the support. It was strange to see the Wicked Witch of the West performing her own little dance moves. Mini Bob Marley clapped his hands while Richard the Lionheart did some kind of body-popping thing.

The dance came to an end. Everyone roared their approval.

'South Crong! South Crong! South Crong!'

Even Maria applauded.

Venetia stepped up to Alma. 'If you like, you don't have to dance. You can surrender right now and enjoy the rest of the party. I'm sure McKay will give you a chicken roll and a jerk chicken pattie.'

'They're all seriously tasty,' cut in McKay. 'Very spicy.'

'Surrender?' Nikesha side-eyed Saira and Venetia. 'Surrender?'

The Nicholas Sisters vs Saira and Venetia

'Surrender to your nineteenth-century moves?' Alma said. 'Do you think we've come all this way on a 109 bus to surrender? Retreat and take a seat! The Nicholas sisters come to rock this beat. In my dictionary, there is no such word as defeat! South Crong, are you ready to take the North Crong heat!'

'DJ Teaspoon!' called out Nikesha. 'Roll the track! Let's give Aladdin and Tennis Barbie the sack!'

The Nicholas sisters adopted a pose. They pressed a button on their heels and their tap shoes lit up with red, gold and green L.E.D. lights. An Afrobeat boomed out of the speakers. They started their routine. Again, perfect timing. They did twirls, spins, complicated step and tap-dancing moves. They performed high leaps and back flips. They used their top hats as props. I looked around. Peeps nodded. I almost felt dizzy just watching them. They finished their dance with another pose as they tossed their tops hats in the air and caught them. Ava was the first to start clapping. Kiran Cassidy and Caroline Stringer joined in before everyone else did.

Then something happened that I never expected.

Saira and Venetia stepped towards the Nicholas sisters and hugged them both.

'That was legend,' Venetia said. 'Can't lie. Proper Broadway moves.'

'You and Saira were legend too.' Alma nodded. 'There's big talent in the South. Can't lie about that.'

'You better believe it,' cut in Liccle Bit.

A Crongton Christmas Party

DJ Teaspoon picked up the microphone. 'Crowd of people,' he said. 'I don't know about you, but I can't separate them. It's gotta be a draw. No need for a North–South Crong war. No one's gonna forget this dance-off in a hurry. It's gonna go down in history in Crongton city! Let's hear it for Venetia, Saira and the Nicholas sisters! I must ask, where are the dancing misters?'

The crowd, including Wendy, hollered and whistled.

'Who's ready for the Crongton Hustle?' rapped DJ Teaspoon.

The Crongton Hustle? What's that? Have I missed something here?

Three lines were formed. DJ Teaspoon played an R&B track and everyone, apart from me, did this line dance thing. Even Wendy and the Nicholas sisters knew the steps and moves.

Why didn't she teach me?

I could only try to follow her as folks cheered and whistled. I accidentally stepped on Jesus Christ's foot.

DJ Teaspoon gave directions, but I couldn't quite follow.

'Two steps to the right.
Step forward.
Two steps back.
Whine your waist like it's made of paste.
Screw up your face like you don't like the taste.
Two steps to the left.
Do the shoulder move.
Flap like a butterfly.
And two steps to the right . . .'

'Where did you learn this?' I asked Wendy.

'That time I went to the youth club,' she replied. 'I thought everyone knew it.'

'I didn't. When did you go to the youth club?' I asked.

'I called for you that evening,' Wendy replied. 'You wasn't in. I wanted you to come with me.'

'You did?'

'Of course I did.' Wendy raised her voice. 'I didn't want to walk back across Crongton Heath on my own.'

'Ahhh.' I smiled. 'You wanted me to be your protector?'

'Er . . . you got that the wrong way around.'

Following the Crongton Hustle, McKay went upstairs to place the patties in the oven. Others followed to get more drinks. Folks came up to me to say what a slamming party I was hosting. I felt noticed. Seen. Not just someone with a funny nickname. *Maybe at school more folks will come up to me and say hi.*

I went up to help McKay.

19

Maria's Blues

'Anything I can do?' I asked McKay when I reached the kitchen.

'I'm good,' replied McKay. 'Patties all in the oven. Maria looked a bit upset when I got up here, though. She was wiping her eyes like she had been crying.'

'Yeah? She's been a bit down cos her fiancé was meant to be in town but he's working extra days on his cruise ship.'

'When I reached the kitchen, she went upstairs.'

'I'll check on her,' I said.

I went upstairs and tapped on Maria's door.

No response. I tried again.

'Is that you, Colin?'

'Yeah. McKay said you looked a bit upset. Is everything OK?'

Silence.

Maria's Blues

'Maria?'

'OK, come in,' she said.

I entered the room. Maria was parked at her dressing table, staring into the mirror. She brushed her hair. Tears filled her eyes.

'Are . . . are you missing Crisanto?' I asked.

'No, it's not him,' she replied. 'Not this time. Don't get me wrong, I'm still mad with him but I'm not crying over him.'

'Then, what is it?'

Maria closed her eyes for a second, as if she was remembering something.

'Just the sight of you and your friends dancing, having such a good time. It triggered something.'

'What . . . what did it trigger?'

Maria wiped her face. She composed herself.

'I was your age once,' she said. 'It wasn't that long ago. I had school friends. Good friends. We had big fun growing up in Manila. We were always in and out of each other's houses or meeting up somewhere after school. We'd stuff our faces with puto cakes and hang out at Rizal Park. You think school days will last forever, then all the fun stops. You must think about careers, jobs, supporting your family. I've been working since I was fifteen. Since then, I haven't seen many friends. Just messages, the odd call. I miss my school days . . . I miss them.'

'I . . . I didn't realise,' I said.

Maria looked at me. 'Why should you? You're young. You're enjoying your school days, your friends. Enjoy every moment, Colin. It'll be over before you're even ready for it.'

'I will,' I said. 'My school friends mean a lot to me. Apart from Wendy, everyone else around here thinks I'm . . . strange.'

'You're not strange, Colin. You just have different things you're interested in. Different things you're good at. It seems most of the young people around here want to go into finance, be the C.E.O. of a top company, or marry someone who's got a job in hedge fund management or something.'

'No one I know is interested in being a landscape artist,' I said.

'Nothing wrong with that,' Maria said. 'Follow your dreams. Design a golf course one day. Isn't that what you want to do?'

'Yeah. I think about it whenever I carry Dad's golf clubs for him at the Biggin Spires course.'

'You were never interested in playing?'

'No, only in where they put the bunkers, cut the greens, plant the bushes, you know, that sort of thing.'

'Does he ever pay you for carrying his clubs?'

I laughed. 'No,' I replied. 'Whenever I asked, Dad would say I live in a nice house, I eat three meals a day and I've got everything I want.'

Someone smacked the letter box.

'Will you be OK?' I asked.

Maria nodded. 'I just need a moment,' she said. 'Go on,

go enjoy your party. Enjoy your friends. These are the days of your lives.'

I skipped downstairs and opened the door. The girl standing in front of me styled a pink coat, pink dress, pink shoes and a long pink wig. Pink Barbie. She even rocked one of those Apple Watches with a pink strap. I had never seen her before.

'Are you gonna let me in or are you just gonna gogglebox me?'

'Er . . . sorry,' I replied. 'My school friends call me Boy from the Hills. My family named me Colin. And you are?'

'Shira,' the girl replied. 'Ava's friend. She said it'd be all right if I came to your rave.'

'Yeah, of course. Come in. Everyone's downstairs.'

'You have a nice house,' she said.

'Thank you.'

I led Shira to the basement. By the time we arrived, DJ Teaspoon was playing a slow jam. Jesus Christ danced with Tina Turner. McKay was with Alma, Mini Bob Marley got groovy with Coco Gauff. Aladdin rocked with Diana Ross. DJ Teaspoon restarted the track and then asked Alma to dance. Wendy stood in a corner. My nerves went viral throughout my body. I sucked in a deep breath and went over to her.

'Wondered where you were,' she said. 'Thought you chickened out.'

'No,' I replied. 'Maria's having issues. She misses home. Misses her friends. She's on her lonesome.'

'Must be hard for her this time of year.'

'Yeah, it is.' I nodded.

'I'll chat to her in a bit, cheer her up. I might invite her to come around and meet the horses. They can be very therapeutic.'

'That's nice of you,' I replied.

She gave me a long look.

'Are you going to ask me to dance?' she asked.

My knees went kinda wobbly, but I don't think she noticed.

'Yeah, of course. May I have this dance, Lady Wendy?'

Wendy pulled a face. 'Let this be a warning,' she said. 'If you ever call me Lady Wendy again, I'll kill you and feed your body to Mr Sutcliffe's pigs!'

I tugged her close to me and we did this slow one-step thing. I looked down to make sure I didn't step on her feet. I glanced over her shoulder and spotted Jonah approaching Pink Barbie. She said yes to his request. I hadn't seen Jonah smile like that since he rolled up at school in Year Seven with a new iPhone. Meanwhile, the Wicked Witch of the West side-eyed Jesus Christ and Tina Turner like she wanted to crucify them.

It was good to see my friends, maybe apart from Juniper, having their best Christmas time.

20

Gatecrashers

'Are you really going to come with me to the races on Boxing Day?' Wendy asked.

'Yeah, why not?' I replied. 'It'll be an experience.'

'You'll have to get up at mad o'clock,' she said. 'It's quite a long drive.'

'It'll get me out of the house. Boxing Day is usually boring around here.'

'Captain Heath has a really good chance of winning,' Wendy said. 'He's just got to stay calm before the race.'

Suddenly, I heard the letter box yapping once again. Whoever it was, they were very impatient.

'You better go see who it is,' Wendy said.

'OK, don't go anywhere.'

'I'll be here.'

'It better not be Mrs Smythe-Watson. She's so nosy.'

A Crongton Christmas Party

I went upstairs, annoyed that whoever it was broke up my slow jam with Wendy. I opened the door.

Oh no!

Vincent Chapman and Donald Thompson stood at the entrance. I tried to push the door closed.

'Let us in, Squire Boy!'

'Guys!' I called out. 'Guys! They've found me!'

First to arrive was Liccle Bit. He helped me hold the door. McKay came next.

'Did our invitation get lost in the post?' Vincent Chapman laughed. 'Let us in! Your place was hard to find.'

'You're not invited!' I shouted.

'Where's your Christian niceness?' Donald Thompson grinned. 'Ain't there no room in the inn for us? It's Christmas.'

'You ain't no Virgin Mary!' I protested.

'There's no room for bandits!' yelled Liccle Bit.

'I swear,' McKay shouted. 'You will never sample one of my mince pies!'

'Open your gates, Squire Boy!'

Jonah, Saira, Venetia and Juniper arrived. We gave my front double-doors a mighty shove and managed to close them. I fumbled in my pocket for my keys and locked the doors.

I breathed out a long sigh.

'How do they know where I live?' I asked. 'How?'

'Someone must've leaked your address,' said Juniper. 'Does your dad have a shotgun or something? Most country peeps do. Let's use it and fire off a warning shot. If that doesn't stop them, aim it at their kneecaps.'

'Er . . . no. My dad doesn't have a shotgun.'

'Can't believe it,' said McKay. 'They sabotaged my dance with Wonder Woman. I was just getting to know her. She wanted to know the ingredients of my chicken pattie.'

'And I only just started rocking with Pink Barbie,' added Jonah. 'She lives in Spenge Ends.'

'Do you think Chapman and Thompson will go home?' asked Venetia. 'South Crong is a long way to trod for nothing.'

We all looked at each other.

'I'm gonna go upstairs and check from my parents' bedroom,' I said. 'I can't have them hanging around and polluting my front garden.'

'We'll follow you,' said Saira.

I switched on the front lawn lights before my friends followed me upstairs. I went to the window that overlooked the front lawn and driveway. Liccle Bit came with me to peer out through the glass.

'Wow!' said Venetia. 'Your parents have a walk-in wardrobe and an en suite bathroom. Gosh! They've got two sinks in there.'

'Look at all the shoes!' said Saira. 'Does your mum wear all of them? And check out the suede boots! Can I try on the tiger-print ones?'

'No!'

'She needs to take a trip to the clothes bank,' said Juniper.

A Crongton Christmas Party

'Boy from the Hills!' Venetia raised her voice. 'I could do a dance routine on your mum's dressing table. It's so long. Is that perfume expensive? Can I spray some on?'

'Guys,' I said. 'We're meant to be looking out for Chapman and Thompson. Remember?'

They joined me at the window. No one was on the lawn. Nor near the front gates.

'They've gone home,' said McKay. 'We can feast in peace.'

'Hold your sleigh rides,' said Liccle Bit. He pointed towards the garage. It wasn't as well-lit as the lawn. We strained our eyes.

Two shadowy figures peered through the window of the garage. They used a phone for a light source.

'Sizzling roses!' I said. 'My dad's DB5 is in there.'

Chapman and Thompson went around to the entrance.

Oh, my daisies! What are they gonna do? Maybe I should've invited them in? What am I saying? They're the school bullies.

Chapman took something out from his jacket. It was murky so I couldn't quite see what it was.

'This is not good,' said Liccle Bit.

'Liberties!' Saira raised her voice. 'He's trying to break in. What are we gonna do?'

Everyone looked at me.

'Call the feds,' said Jonah. 'You got no choice. Tell them you've got bad-minded people about to jack your car.'

'They'll take forever to come,' said Venetia. 'We gotta do something.'

Gatecrashers

The garage door had a small padlock on it. Dad never felt the need to have a proper security system because we'd never had a break-in.

We watched Chapman manage to open the door and step inside. Thompson followed him in.

I imagined them driving Dad's precious DB5 on a cadazy joyride through the woods. They'd crash into trees and hit rocks. Might even fall over a cliff. My heart walloped my chest.

'We can't just stand here and look,' said Saira.

I'm not sure where it came from, but rage erupted in my veins. I didn't even realise my fists were clenched. I hot-stepped out of my parents' bedroom and bounced downstairs. I opened the front door and zoomed towards the garage. I didn't know who was behind me. 'Chapman!' I screamed. 'You're a dead man!'

I entered the garage. A broken padlock was on the floor. The smell of polish hit my nose. Chapman had switched on the light. It flickered on and off. I couldn't quite believe what my eyes told me. I came to a sudden halt as shock blazed through me.

Chapman was grooving a squiggly line on the bonnet of the DB5 with a front door key. The sound of it was like an eagle's claw scraping down a blackboard. He might as well have scratched my nerves with it. Thompson giggled. He had a long screwdriver in his left hand. He wielded it like he was going to use it to defend himself. My head felt warm. My heartbeat raced. My legs felt funny. The world seemed a blurry place. I sensed the presence of my friends.

'That's just evil,' said McKay.

'There's more of us than them!' shouted Liccle Bit. 'Let's delete them!'

'Yeah!' roared Saira. 'Don't let them get away with it.'

I felt dizzy. Everything seemed to happen in slow motion. Suddenly, my feet were unsteady. I banged my head on something. The last thing I heard was Bossi barking.

21

The Search for Bossi

I opened my eyes. I found myself lying down on my black leather sofa in the front lounge. My hair and face were wet. Many eyes stared at me. I heard music playing from the basement.

Oh yes, I remembered. I was hosting a party. I had danced with Wendy. *Was that a dream?*

DJ Teaspoon rapped something on the microphone. Chapman and Thompson broke into our garage. They damaged Dad's DB5.

Oh no! It was all too real.

'I told you he's not dead,' said Juniper. 'Not yet, anyway.'

Maybe I'll be better off dead before my parents find out.

'He fainted,' said Venetia. 'Give him some water.'

I sat up. My vision was a bit blurry. McKay handed me a cup of water. I took three sips.

'What happened?' I asked.

'Bossi happened,' replied Liccle Bit.

'What do you mean?' I wondered.

'I let loose your Jurassic hound,' said Jonah. 'I opened the side gate, let Bossi out, and he hot-pawed straight to the garage. Chapman and Thompson took one look at him and they rocket-toed away like a T-Rex wanted to fang them. Not sure if they knew where they were going in the dark, but they ran towards the Shrublands Road.'

'Dad's DB5!' I raised my voice. 'Did you see the scratch?'

My friends looked at each other.

'So, I didn't imagine it?' I asked.

Saira shook her head. 'I'm so sorry that happened. As McKay said, it's just evil, hateful behaviour.'

'They should pay for the damage,' said Venetia.

'Fat chance of that,' replied Juniper. 'Send them to prison! Or cut off their fingers! That's what they used to do in the olden days.'

'My dad's gonna kill me and then bury me under a bunker,' I said. 'This is *not* good! My life is over.'

'Fling some more water over him,' said Juniper. 'He's panicking again.'

'Calm down,' said Venetia. 'It's not the end of the world.'

'It is!' I insisted. 'You don't know how much that ride means to my pops.'

'Maybe . . . maybe I can do something,' said Liccle Bit.

'What can you do?' I asked. 'Find a good place to bury my body? Say something nice at my funeral?'

'No, no,' Liccle Bit replied. 'Let me go home and get my art kit. I think I might be able to use some filler, smooth it down and mix a few colours to get the right shade. It's a long shot but worth a try.'

'It won't be the same,' I said. 'I'm doomed.'

'It's worth a go,' said Juniper. 'Your dad might not notice it.'

'If a flea took a crap on his DB5, he'd notice it,' I said.

'When is he due back?' Saira asked.

'Tomorrow,' I replied. 'My execution day.'

'I start work on it tonight,' said Liccle Bit.

'Until Liccle Bit comes back,' McKay said. 'Let's munch on patties. They're ready.'

I sank another cup of water as McKay went to fetch me a pattie. It was meaty, spicy. The yellow pastry flakes melted on my tongue.

Delicious. It might be my last meal.

Maria came over. Concern marked her forehead. 'How are you feeling?' she asked.

'OK, I think,' I replied.

'Sorry to bring you more problems,' Maria said. 'But Bossi's missing. I checked in the garden and he's not there.'

'Didn't he come back?'

Maria shook her head. 'Who were those horrible boys? Did you invite them?'

'No, I did not,' I replied. 'They're school bullies. They gave me grief in Year Seven and Eight. Now they're giving me grief at my own gates.'

A Crongton Christmas Party

'You're going to have to look for Bossi,' Maria said. 'Otherwise, Mrs Utili will not enjoy her port on New Year's Eve.'

'Who's gonna come with me to search for Bossi?' I asked. I searched all eyes.

'In this dark?' Jonah asked. 'Are you cadazy? We don't know what's out there in those woods.'

'I don't think we'll find any vampires or dinosaurs,' said Saira. 'We're *all* going to help you find Bossi.'

'Yep,' said McKay. 'But not until I finish my pattie. If I say so myself, these are the best homemade patties ever baked in South Crong. No doubt about it.'

No one disagreed.

'While you look for Bossi,' said Liccle Bit, 'I'll go home and get my kit.'

'Do you think it'll work?' I asked.

'Anyone got any better ideas?' Liccle Bit asked. No one replied.

Ten minutes later, I left my gates with my friends behind me. As we started on the Shrublands Road, I shone a torch in front of us. My friends used the lights on their phones. A cold chill was in the air. Stars sprinkled the night sky.

What else is gonna go wrong tonight? Don't tempt fate, Colin.

'I usually take Bossi for his walks in the woods,' I said. 'We'll leave the road when we get to the Falcon Ridge path.'

'Peeps go missing on that path,' said Jonah. 'I'm not lying.'

'I'm sure we'll be OK,' said Venetia. 'After all, we have Bob Marley, Aladdin, Robin Hood, Richard the Lionheart and the Wicked Witch of the West to protect us.'

'Don't want to panic anybody,' said Juniper. 'But Chapman and Thompson are still out there somewhere. We might stumble on their dead bodies. Wasn't someone brutally murdered in these woods a few years ago?'

'That's not funny, Juniper,' Jonah replied.

We entered the woods. I couldn't see the sky. The air tasted different. Jonah kept close to me. He kept on glancing over his shoulder. I didn't want to say it, but someone *was* killed in these woods ten years ago. A man murdered his wife. Mrs Corkstone. She lived around the corner from Wendy. Her husband buried the body along with her pet poodle, Frenchie. The feds arrested him seven months later.

Better not tell Jonah. He'll freak.

'Bossi! Bossi! Bossi!'

No response.

'I can't believe that one minute, I'm slow-jamming with Pink Barbie, and the next minute, I'm out here in the woods,' moaned Jonah. 'There's bears out here.'

'Who told you that?' I asked.

'Devon Sinclair,' Jonah replied.

'Devon Sinclair is always making up stuff,' said McKay. 'Don't listen to him.'

'He might not be wrong,' said Jonah. 'Say he's right? I don't wanna be mauled by a bear. And they don't just eat the flesh, they eat bones, lips and fingernails too.'

Venetia laughed. 'There are no bears in the Crongton Woods,' she said. 'Next you'll be saying there's Big Foots out here as well.'

'What's a Big Foot?' asked Saira.

'Big Foots?' replied McKay. 'They kinda look like Chewbacca from Star Wars but three times the size. Oh, and obviously they've got mega-size feet. They live up hills and mountains.'

'I don't wanna be squashed by a Big Foot,' said Jonah.

'That'll be very messy,' giggled Juniper. 'Proper messy like an undercooked Bolognese.'

'Eeeeewwwww!' squealed Venetia.

'Can we call out for Bossi again?' I asked.

'Bossi! Bossi! Bossi!'

'He might've been crushed by a Big Foot,' wondered Jonah. 'You'll have to use a spoon to scoop him into a dog coffin.'

'I'm gonna use my big foot and kick you with it if you keep on going on about imaginary monsters,' threatened Saira.

'Bossi! Bossi! Bossi!'

'He might have been flown away by flying monkeys,' laughed Juniper. 'And taken to some weird castle in the wilderness. Or aliens. Aliens might've captured him. Bossi could be in a spaceship heading towards the planet Zod.'

'Where's planet Zod?' asked Jonah.

'The other side of Pluto,' replied Juniper.

'I think we're letting our imaginations run away with ourselves,' said Venetia.

'Wait a minute!' said McKay. 'Why didn't I think of it before? Bossi loves his duck meat, right?'

'You're not wrong there,' I replied. 'And his rabbit meat. Bossi's a strange hound.'

'I am not hunting rabbits in this dark,' said Jonah. 'No freaking way!'

'I think they hibernate in the winter,' I said.

'Let me go back to the house and microwave the duck meat that was left over,' suggested McKay. 'We'll take it out here, and Bossi might sniff and come and get it.'

'He might not sniff it,' said Jonah. 'Bossi could be miles and miles away. He could be in Monks Orchard or Nobbler Fields by now.'

'Well, thank you, Mr Positive,' said Saira.

'It's worth a try,' I said. 'Remember, dogs can smell from a long way away.'

I led my friends back to the house. McKay warmed up already cooked duck meat in the microwave and placed it on a paper plate. I can't lie. The smell of it was good. We hit the Shrublands Road again before following the Falcon Ridge path.

'Bossi! Bossi! Bossi!'

'This is not gonna work,' said Jonah. 'Can't we go back to the party and search in the morning?'

'Bossi! Bossi! Bossi!'

I heard a faint noise. At first, I thought it was the breeze passing through the branches. But no, it was a galloping sound.

'Bossi! Bossi! Bossi!'

Before I could call out again, Bossi sprang out of the darkness and almost flattened McKay. Duck meat went all over the ground, but Bossi didn't care. He sniffed it and gobbled it up. He even licked the paper plate.

'Now I know how to find McKay if he gets lost,' joked Juniper.

I hugged Bossi and he slobbered my face.

Roasting acorns! I smell of duck! This won't be good if I have another slow jam with Wendy.

'Whatever you do,' Venetia said to me. '*Don't* take Bossi for a walk to Miller's Pond. The ducks there will soon be extinct if Bossi gets a sniff of them.'

'That'll be messy,' added Juniper.

'Can we go back to the house now?' asked Jonah.

'Do we have to?' asked Juniper. 'I've always wondered what you might see in the woods when it's dark. The bats might come out and play.'

'NO!' everyone replied.

22

English Tea and Condensed Milk

It had just gone 6.15 p.m. We made it back to the house. I looked forward to another dance with Wendy – if she was still there.

Would she have left without saying goodbye? Surely not!

'The chicken rolls!' said McKay as we approached my gates. 'I need to put them in the oven. We'll snack on those when we get back inside.'

'Sounds good to me,' said Saira. 'I'll help you serve.'

'Bossi can stay inside,' I said. 'I'm not leaving him in the garden.'

Jonah pulled a face. 'I hope he doesn't eat peeps the way he sinks duck meat,' he warned.

We entered my house. I looked to the right towards the kitchen with Bossi in tow. Someone was sitting with Maria.

Stresses and curses! Mrs Smythe-Watson.

A Crongton Christmas Party

Her deerstalker hat crowned her head. She wore her green wellington boots. She sipped a hot drink from one of Mum's expensive china mugs. She nibbled one of McKay's mince pies.

'You go downstairs,' I said to my friends. 'Let me see what Mrs Smythe-Watson wants.'

I joined Mrs Smythe-Watson in the kitchen. She studied her tea like there was a slug swimming in it. She turned to Maria. 'Are you sure you put condensed milk in here?' she asked.

'Yes, I did,' replied Maria.

'And two and a half sugars? Not three?'

'Two and a half sugars like you asked me,' said Maria.

'Did you give it a good stir?'

'Yes, I stirred it,' said Maria.

Mrs Smythe-Watson looked at me. 'Young Colin,' she said. 'I was enjoying my evening glass of malt whisky, looking out to my front garden as I do.'

'Yes?' I nodded. 'Not much of a view this time of night.'

'When all of a sudden' – Mrs Smythe-Watson raised her voice – 'two thugs climbed over my fence and ran across my front lawn. I was very alarmed, let me tell you. My husband's not at home. I could have been in all sorts of peril. Who knows what could have become of me.'

'I'm sorry to hear that,' I said.

'I haven't finished yet,' Mrs Smythe-Watson cut me off. 'To make matters worse, this huge dog chased these boys across my lawn. It was very traumatic. I had a good mind to call the police. I didn't know what was going on.'

'That's a good thing, isn't it?' I offered. 'At least the dog got rid of your garden bandits.'

'*Don't* get clever with me, young Colin,' snapped Mrs Smythe-Watson. 'I imagine these hooligans attended your party.'

'I didn't invite them!' I protested. 'They're gatecrashers.'

'Hmmm. All the same. This is a quiet community. We never have any trouble.'

'Never have any trouble!' I repeated. 'Mr Corkstone killed his wife and buried her in the hills. He wasn't exactly a friendly neighbour.'

'Yeah, well. That was unfortunate. I'll be speaking to your parents about this evening.'

'Do you have to?'

'Yes, they should be informed what occurs here when you're left to your own devices. You should choose your friends more wisely.'

'I didn't invite them!' I repeated.

'Don't raise your voice to me, young Colin. Also, the dog is your responsibility. I hope you can keep it secure. Instead of allowing it to run wild. Mrs Utili should put that thing down.'

'He was chasing away those gatecrashers.'

Mrs Smythe-Watson side-eyed me like she didn't believe a word I said. She finished her mince pie and stood up. She dabbed her lips with a hanky. 'When are your parents back?' she asked.

'Tomorrow,' I replied.

A Crongton Christmas Party

'I'll look out for them,' she said. 'In the meantime, try to control your guests.'

Mrs Smythe-Watson marched towards the front door, opened it and left. I puffed out a long sigh. For a short second, I wished all of Santa's reindeers, sleigh included, fell on her from a great height.

'I wasn't going to let her in,' said Maria. 'But she kept on knocking.'

'What am I gonna do, Maria?' I asked. 'Mrs Smythe-Watson is gonna spill everything to my parents and that scratch on Dad's DB5 is still there. I'll probably be grounded forever.'

Maria placed a hand on my shoulder. 'Your parents are not home yet,' she said. 'You have a lovely girl waiting for you downstairs. My woman sense tells me she's keen on you. The DJ is still playing music. Go on! Go downstairs and enjoy the rest of your party. Who knows when you're going to have big fun again?'

23

Missing Mistletoe

When I reached the basement, Wendy was bubbling and dancing with my friends as DJ Teaspoon played some R&B jams. The Nicholas sisters were still there, along with Pink Barbie, Wonder Woman, Tina Turner and the rest of my guests. I joined in the dancing. I wasn't sure what I was doing, but no one seemed to care.

Jesus Christ stepped up to me. 'I'm having a New Year's Eve ting at my place,' he said. 'Why don't you and Wendy come?'

'Yeah, why not,' I replied.

'I haven't got a DJ,' Jesus Christ explained. 'And it's not fancy dress. We're just gonna see in the New Year, you know, sink some food, watch TV, listen out for the chimes of Big Ben. There'll be a lot of Doritos, crisps, peanuts and soft drinks.'

'I'm there.' I nodded. 'Thanks for inviting me.'

A Crongton Christmas Party

Jesus Christ resumed dancing with Tina Turner.

Oh my gosh! No one from school has ever invited me to a party before. Yeah, I've been around my friends' houses. But Kiran Cassidy! One of the most popular guys in school. This is mega.

I felt like somebody. I had to tell Wendy.

'Wendy! Wendy! Guess what?'

'Guess what?' she repeated. 'Mrs Smythe-Watson revealed that she's a real witch?'

'No, no, no,' I replied. 'We've been invited to Kiran's rave on New Year's Eve.'

'Who's Kiran?'

'The guy dressed up as Jesus.'

'Oh, yes.' Wendy nodded. 'That'll be cool. Maybe he can turn the Coke Zero into wine.'

I laughed. 'Never drank wine,' I admitted.

'Don't your parents let you have a glass of wine on Christmas Day?' Wendy asked.

'Nope,' I replied. 'They let me have this fizzy cider thing.'

'Don't worry.' Wendy grinned. 'I'll pour you a glass on Boxing Day. Just half a glass, mind you. My dad's OK with that.'

'Er . . . yeah. Why not?'

'Can you walk me home?' Wendy asked. 'Got to get up early in the morning and ride out Captain Heath.'

'Yeah, of course.'

We climbed the stairs, said goodbye to Maria and stepped out. We heard the bassline of the music at the front of my gates.

Missing Mistletoe

I'm sure Mrs Smythe-Watson will complain about that.

I could just make out a low mist settling over the Heath. We turned left on to the Heath Road. It was just after 7.30 p.m. Everything was quiet.

Now it was just Wendy and me, I wasn't sure what to say to her. I felt proper nervous. Especially as we had danced up close.

Is Maria right? Is she really keen on me for real? Say she's wrong? I might make a super duper idiot of myself. She might have her eye on someone else. Maybe one of those horsey folks. Girls my age always prefer someone a year or so older. Especially the pretty ones. Did I spray on enough deodorant before the party?

'Nice party,' Wendy said. 'You've got some cool friends. The dance clash was awesome. I recorded it. I can't wait till I show my friends at school.'

'Yeah, it was an ace party, wasn't it? McKay served up some neat food, the DJ was on point and Mrs Smythe-Watson didn't call the army reserves on us. Mind you, she still might do that.'

Wendy giggled. 'Is it true her husband spends most of his time in his man cave?'

'Yep.' I nodded. 'I think he sleeps there too.'

'Don't blame him.'

Wendy rubbed her hands and then she linked her right arm with my left. A tingle sparked through my body.

She's just cold. That's all. It probably means nothing.

We approached Wendy's place. It was a converted stone-built farmhouse. It had an old-school chimney on top.

Wendy's dad had built an extension for the stables. I sniffed hay and horse crap. There was a lamp above Wendy's front door. Three well-worn concrete steps led up to it. A brown bristled mat said Welcome. Christmas fairy lights lit up the fake-frosted windows.

'Are you gonna come in?' Wendy asked. 'I usually make myself a cocoa before I go upstairs to my room. I've got some chocolate-chip cookies too. I made them yesterday.'

'Er . . . no. I better get back. Liccle Bit will be back soon to try to repair the scratch on the DB5. And I'm the host of the party, remember. I also must make sure that Bossi doesn't fang anybody. I don't think he will. He's quite tame.'

Blazing daisies! Did I say that the right way? I hope she's not disappointed.

'And a good host you are,' Wendy said. 'Don't worry. Bossi's cool. I really enjoyed myself. It was nice dressing up as Rachael Blackmore. One day, I'll win the Grand National too.'

'I'm sure you will.' I nodded. 'Just don't ride a horse over one of my golf courses.'

'I'll see you at mad o'clock on Boxing Day morning.'

'What time is mad o'clock?'

'Six-thirty . . . ish.'

'That's not so bad.'

Wendy went inside. I stood on the step for a moment. I wondered if Wendy and me were getting closer or if I was still in the friend zone. The door opened again. Without warning, Wendy came out and kissed me on the cheek.

Missing Mistletoe

'There's . . . there's no mistletoe,' I said.

'Mistletoe? Who needs mistletoe? That's for boring Christmas films.'

'Oh . . . OK.'

'Merry Christmas, Colin. Thanks for walking me home.'

'No worries. Merry Christmas to you too.'

'And a happy new year.'

'Er . . . Wendy,' I said. 'Are we . . . are we, like, an item now?'

'We better be.'

She smiled and closed the door. My heart sang. At least I think it did.

She kissed me! Sizzling chestnuts! She went inside and came back out just to kiss me. This is mega. Wendy's now my official girlfriend. Must get back so I can broadcast this breaking news.

I jumped down from Wendy's steps and bounced my way along the pavement.

I have a girlfriend! Yes! I bet Vincent Chapman and Donald Thompson don't have a girl. The universe is all good. One day there will be world peace. I might even watch a romcom. Who cares if Dad grounds me. Screw his DB5! Maybe I should've stepped inside for a cocoa and choc-chip cookies?

I made it home in ten minutes. The light was switched on in the garage. I headed there.

24

Sandpaper and Silver Paint

Liccle Bit was crouched over the bonnet of the DB5. He gripped a small block of wood wrapped up in fine sandpaper. He studied the scratch on the car like it was a demon he wanted to expel.

'How's it going?' I asked.

'The filler dried quick,' he replied. He ran his finger over the damaged area. 'Just making sure it's smooth enough before I mix the paint.'

'Thanks for doing this,' I said. 'Really appreciate it.'

'Just hope it works. Even if it doesn't, at least we tried.'

Carefully, Liccle Bit applied the sandpaper again. He blew away the dust. He examined the bonnet once more.

'That should do it,' he said. 'Now to mix the paint.'

I watched him stir white and black paint in a small pot. He used a skinny brush. He had steady hands.

Sandpaper and Silver Paint

'A bit more white,' Liccle Bit said to himself. 'I'm looking for that silvery-grey shade.'

'Wendy kissed me,' I blurted out.

Liccle Bit stood up and turned to me. A dose of silver-grey paint was on his chin. 'Seriously? No jokes?'

'I'm not lying,' I said. 'I walked her to her door, she went inside. And then she came back out and kissed me. I was proper shocked.'

'Where did she kiss you?' Liccle Bit asked. 'The forehead doesn't count.'

'On the cheek,' I replied.

'Where on the cheek? High up on the cheekbone, close to your ear or near the mouth?'

'In the middle,' I said.

'My granny kisses me on the middle of the cheek,' Liccle Bit said.

'It wasn't a granny kiss,' I argued. 'You should've been there. It was proper authentic. Like at the end of romcom films. I'm going racing with her on Boxing Day.'

'Racing? What? Horses?'

'Yeah, one of her horses, Captain Heath, is running over the jumps. I see it as a date thing.'

Liccle Bit concentrated his eyes. He brushed the silver-grey paint over the scratch. He stood back and admired his work.

'What do you think?' I asked.

'Racing?' he repeated. 'Not a proper date. A proper date is like going to the movies or taking a girl to the Cheesecake Lounge.'

'Wendy's into her horses,' I said. 'She's not a movie kinda girl. More the outside type.'

Venetia entered the garage. She inspected Liccle Bit's handiwork. 'That's not too bad,' she said. 'You have to look really hard to tell the difference.'

'Yeah.' Liccle Bit nodded. 'Boy from the Hills' pops won't notice a damn thing. Just got to polish it when it's dry. By the way, Boy from the Hills got breaking news.'

'What breaking news?' Venetia asked.

Liccle Bit and I swapped a glance. I got a bit tongue-tied. Venetia stared at me. I felt my face roasting with embarrassment.

'Wendy kissed him,' revealed Liccle Bit. 'In the middle of the cheek.'

'That's great!' Venetia said. 'I knew she was on you. It was soooo obvious.'

'It was?' I asked.

'Course it was,' said Venetia. 'Remember you telling me that she's always surprising you, turning up at your gates.'

'Yeah,' I said. 'Sometimes she just turns up out of the blue.'

'That means she's on you.' Venetia nodded. 'And has been for the longest time.'

'But she only kissed him on the cheek,' said Liccle Bit.

'She confirmed we are an item,' I replied.

'Doesn't matter that it was only on the cheek,' said Venetia. 'I'm glad for you. I just have one tip.'

'One tip?' I asked. 'What's that?'

'When you take her out to somewhere like the Cheesecake Lounge,' Venetia advised, 'make a bit of an effort.'

'What do you mean make a bit of an effort?' I asked.

'She means don't turn up for your date looking like you just wrestled with a pig or taken a roll down Falcon's Ridge,' Liccle Bit advised. 'Wear something decent and do something with your hair.'

'Yes, definitely do something with your hair,' Venetia agreed. 'Like how you came to my church the other day. I hardly recognised you. I thought you had a better-looking brother.'

'I will,' I said. I couldn't kill my grin. 'I've got a girlfriend now. Some folks at school won't believe it. I can hardly believe it.'

Liccle Bit rolled his eyes as Venetia clapped. 'Good for you!'

25

Behind Enemy Lines

'I nearly forgot,' said Venetia. 'The Nicholas sisters are getting ready to leave. They wanted to say goodbye to you.'

'They did?' I replied. 'That's polite of them.'

'They're not so bad when you get to know them,' Venetia added.

'Despite them coming from North Crong?' Liccle Bit cut in. He shook his head. 'I still don't trust them.'

I followed Venetia out of the garage. We entered the house just as Maria was wrapping patties and chicken rolls in silver foil for the Nicholas sisters to take home.

'Thanks for having us,' said Nikesha.

'And thanks for giving us food to take home,' added Alma.

'You're welcome,' said Maria. 'Snacks for your bus ride.'

Alma spotted Venetia and me.

'We've stepped to your ends for a dance clash,' Alma said to Venetia. 'How about you bouncing up to our lands for a return match?'

'To North Crong?' I raised my tones.

'Yes!' Nikesha nodded. 'To North Crong. It's not the other side of the world. Just a 109 bus ride. Not scared, are you?'

Jonah appeared from the basement. He stepped towards the kitchen and poured himself a Coke Zero.

'You're not gonna mouse out on us, are you?' challenged Alma.

'I'll never mouse out,' replied Venetia. 'Any place, anytime, anywhere.'

'Mouse out on what?' Jonah asked.

'The Nicholas sisters have challenged Venetia to step to their ends for a rematch,' I explained.

'In North Crong?' Jonah asked. 'Did I hear right? That's like going to Mordor in *Lord of the Rings*.'

'In North Crong.' I nodded. 'You heard correct.'

'Where in North Crong?' Venetia asked.

'The youth club,' Nikesha replied. 'We have dance night on Thursdays.'

'You're on!' said Venetia. 'Saira and I will bring it.'

I glanced at Jonah. He looked like he had just swallowed a half-cooked toad.

'The youth club is closed during the Christmas holidays,' Alma said. 'But when it reopens, we'll set it up. We'll get a good crowd in and a top-ranking DJ. You can choose the beats.'

'No worries,' said Venetia. 'Until then, make sure you practise hard.'

'And you and Saira practise harder,' replied Nikesha. 'Trust me, you won't be stepping home with any flowers.'

I opened the door for them, and the Nicholas sisters left.

'Are you cadazy?' snapped Jonah. 'North Crong Youth Club? Isn't that the place where you have to pass through metal detectors to get in? Peeps get deleted in that club every week, and that's North Crong folk. What do you think they'll do to *us*? Our parents won't recognise our bodies.'

'It's just a dance clash,' said Venetia. 'We'll be cool.'

'Where's your memory?' asked Jonah. 'Every time we step near North Crong, we barely escape with our lives. I don't think my stress levels can take another mission there.'

'You don't have to come,' said Venetia.

Jonah thought about it.

'I'll be there,' said Liccle Bit, who had just come through the front door.

'And I'll be there,' I said. 'Can't be worse than waiting for my pops to find out what happened to his DB5.'

'I done a good job!' said Liccle Bit. 'Boy from the Hills' pops is not gonna notice a diddly. Just make sure you give the bonnet a serious polish in the morning.'

'Anyone want more chicken rolls?' Maria offered. 'I must get the recipe from McKay. The flavour and spices are delicious.'

We all sank more chicken rolls. McKay had come up from the basement. He used a paper towel to wipe the sweat from his forehead.

'Been dancing,' he explained. He grinned like the happiest guy in the world as he watched us sample his chicken rolls. 'Next time I'm charging for my party catering services,' he said. 'No more freeness. I'm just toooo good.'

26

Spider-Man Always Knocks Twice

Forty-five minutes later, everyone had left. Jonah and Liccle Bit helped me carry the pool table back into place. Venetia and Saira collected all the empty paper cups and plates. They placed them in a black rubbish bag. Juniper washed up stuff in the kitchen. DJ Teaspoon was the last to leave after one final coffee.

'I'm getting pure love on my socials,' he said. 'The dance clash is going viral. I'm getting nuff likes and smiley faces. Peeps are already contacting me about DJing their gigs. Maybe I can convince Kiran to let me rock some Afrobeats at his New Year's Eve ting. That'll be the bomb.'

'You done good,' I said. 'Folks were bubbling all evening. Thanks for playing.'

Maria and I sat at the kitchen table. She sipped Prosecco

from a paper cup. Her eyes were closing. I munched on another chicken roll. It had a jerky, peppery taste to it.

Maybe McKay could do the food at Kiran's New Year ting.

'Well?' Maria asked. 'What happened when you walked Wendy home? I noticed that you came back with a big glow on your face.'

I couldn't delete my grin. 'She kissed me!' I said. 'Yeah, I didn't expect it.'

Maria slapped the table. 'I told you! I knew she was keen on you. She always looks out of sorts when she stops by and you're not at home.'

'She does?'

'Yes, her head drops. Then she slowly leaves. *"Make sure you tell Colin I've stopped by"* she'd say.'

'I better buy her a Christmas present,' I said. 'There's only one day of shopping left. What do I buy her?'

'Keep it simple,' suggested Maria. 'You just became an item a few minutes ago. Buy her a Christmas card and write a nice message in it.'

'Is that all?'

'Yes. As I said, keep it simple. It's what you say that is important.'

'What shall I say?' I asked.

'How did you feel when she kissed you?'

I thought about it. Again, I couldn't get rid of my smile. I closed my eyes for half a second and relived the kiss. 'Like bolts of goodness were shooting through me. Instead of walking home, I think I floated. It's like I've been overdosed with happiness.'

'Say something like that,' said Maria. 'Say she makes you happy, makes you smile. Say you love her company.'

'And that's all?'

'That's all. I don't think Wendy's the type of girl who likes big gestures.'

'So, no perfume? Flowers?'

'Too early for flowers. Save that for anniversaries or birthdays.'

The letter box rapped again.

'Who could that be?' I asked.

'Hopefully not Mrs Smythe-Watson,' Maria replied. 'I don't think I'm in a good enough state to brew another cup of tea to her liking.'

For a moment, I hesitated.

Please don't let it be Vincent Chapman and Donald Thompson.

Rap-a-pap-pap!

I went to answer the door.

Spider-Man stood before me. I could only see his eyes and lips.

'Who . . . who?'

'Devon . . . Devon Sinclair. I've come for the party.'

Devon pulled off his mask. He performed a short version of the Crongton Hustle. 'I'm ready to bubble! Where's everyone at?'

'Everyone's gone home,' I said. 'DJ Teaspoon left about forty-five minutes ago.'

'No jokes?' Devon said. 'I thought it was an all-night thing. Someone said you had the house to yourself. No parents. I saw DJ Teaspoon's socials. Everyone was fizzing. The dance clash was mega. Between you and me, I'd say the Nicholas sisters won. I have to give them top ratings.'

'Don't let Venetia hear you say that.'

'It's just my opinion. She'll be cool with it.'

'Er . . . do you want a mince pie?' I offered.

'Yeah.' Devon nodded. 'Give me an extra one for the road. I spent most of the day visiting relatives. Can't believe I missed everything.'

I warmed up two mince pies in the microwave. Devon munched one before he left. 'Let me know if you have any more raves.'

Maria's eyes were closed.

'I'll have to face the music tomorrow,' I said.

Maria opened one tired eye. She was about to say something but she changed her mind.

'Do you know what time my parents are coming home?'

'I think they said lunchtime,' replied Maria. 'Stop worrying. What's the worst they can do to you?'

'Ground me. I'm meant to be going horseracing with Wendy on Boxing Day, and we've been invited to a New Year's Eve party. I might have to delete all of that from my plans. My Christmas is broken.'

'There'll be other dates, other parties.'

'But me and Wendy have just got together.'

'It'll work out,' Maria insisted. 'Be patient. We're both tired. I'm turning in. You should too. Bossi needs to go on his walk in the morning.'

'Thank you for everything. Goodnight, Maria.'

I sank one more mince pie before I went upstairs. Bossi followed me. He curled up near the foot of my bed.

What am I gonna say to my parents? Mrs Smythe-Watson will definitely spill. They're gonna ground my partying ass. I hope Wendy can still visit me.

27

Awaiting Punishment

Maria cooked me poached eggs, bacon, hashbrowns and baked beans for breakfast. I flung some brown sauce on it to give it a bit of a boot. I chased that down with a strawberry and blueberry smoothie that she had blended.

Maria spoils me. I should have bought her a Christmas present.

'Don't worry,' she said. 'It's Christmas Eve! I'm sure your parents won't overreact to your party.'

'Don't know about that,' I replied. 'Remember, they're hearing about it from Mrs Smythe-Watson. She makes everything sound ten times more toxic. She's probably chatting to them right now.'

'You take Bossi for his walk,' she suggested. 'And I'll vacuum downstairs, make everything look tidy.'

'Thank you, Maria,' I said. 'Don't know what I'd do without you in my corner.'

I washed up my plate and glass before securing the lead on Bossi's collar.

It was just after 8 a.m. It was a bright morning, just a few clouds in the sky. I decided to take Bossi up the Falcon Ridge path.

That'll tire him out.

My first text of the morning came from Jonah.

Did shira give you her phone number?

I replied quickly.

No

Jonah called me.

'I need to give her a ding,' he said. 'I think she's on me. Did you see her dancing with me? Our cheeks touched. And you know what? She never pulled away.'

'Er . . . yes, I did. Don't you think it's a bit early-morning-dot-com to call her? It's eight-fifteen on Christmas Eve.'

'Maybe you're right,' Jonah said. 'Perhaps eight-thirty will be good.'

'Remember, she's Ava's friend. Obviously, *she* knows Shira's number.'

'Yes, yes, I'll give McKay a ding so he can get Shira's number from Ava.'

'Just don't go on like a hound,' I advised.

'A hound? I never go on like a hound. When you meet a

girl like Shira, you've got to act fast, man. She's got brains, she's pretty, and she's into her athletics. Brothers are probably stepping up to her every day. And a few sisters too. I don't want any other kerb rat to block me. I wanna invite her to Kiran's New Year's Eve ting.'

'At least wait till after ten.'

'All right, then. I'll tell you what happens.'

'Good luck!'

Jonah killed the call. Next to give me a ding was Saira.

'How is everything?' she asked. 'Is your pops home?'

'Not yet,' I replied. 'I've got a few hours till I get my sentence.'

'The car's not too bad,' Saira said. 'Liccle Bit done a good job.'

'But Mrs Smythe-Watson's gonna leak everything to my parents.'

'Maybe we can get Juniper to take her out before she leaks on your ass.'

'Don't tell Juniper that,' I laughed. 'She'd probably delete her for real.'

'Merlene and I had a good talk on the way home last night,' Saira said. 'No one really said anything about us. No hateful comments or messed-up looks.'

'You see?' I said. 'You had nothing to worry about. Everyone will be cool with you and Merlene.'

'That's the easy part,' Saira replied. 'How am I gonna tell my family that I'm dating a girl? It'll be bad enough for them to find out I'm dating full stop. My brother won't love it and my aunt will have a seizure.'

'Maybe keep it on a low profile for the time being,' I advised. 'Just enjoy getting to know Merlene.'

'But I don't wanna hide who I am,' Saira said. 'It'll be like lying.'

'It's like knowing there's a storm coming at the end of the week,' I said. 'You can't do anything about mad weather, but you can enjoy the calm days before nature does its thing.'

'I . . . I hear that,' Saira said.

'Have you two got any missions planned over the holidays?'

'Yeah, we're going ice-skating on Saturday.'

'That's all good,' I said.

'It is,' replied Saira. 'But I can't skate.'

'She'll teach you.'

'I hope I won't embarrass myself.'

'Wendy's taking me horseracing on Boxing Day,' I said. 'If my parents don't ground my backside.'

'They won't ground you.'

'They definitely will,' I insisted. 'You don't know them. And I'll probably miss out on Kiran's New Year's Eve rave.'

'Don't get so negative,' Saira said. 'You should be proper happy. You and Wendy are an item now. Your parents can't sabotage that.'

'And your family can't mash up your thing with Merlene.'

Silence.

'Saira? You still there?'

'Yeah, I'm still here. My family can mess things up more than you can imagine.'

'You'll be OK.'

'I hope so. Anyway, good luck with your parents. I'm gonna ding Venetia. See if she's got up yet. She said to me last night that she wants me to go last-minute-dot-com shopping with her. She still needs to buy the twins their Christmas presents.'

'Good luck with that,' I said. 'I'll chat to you later.'

'Bye.'

I killed the call. There was a text message from McKay.

Did anyone give my baking low ratings?

I gave him a ring.

'Everyone loved it. Especially the spicy-flavoured chicken rolls. Did you put jerk seasoning in it?'

'I sure did! And I put a dose of chilli in it too. Next time I'm gonna fry my own version of fried chicken. Party folks gonna have to pay me to cater from now on. I'm officially a pro.'

'How much are you gonna charge?' I asked.

'Good question. Let me think on that one. Good luck with your dad's DB5 – hope he doesn't notice anything. Don't tell Liccle Bit I said so, but he's top ranking when it comes to art.'

'Yep. You're not wrong. He might've saved my ass.'

'I've got to head out today,' McKay said. 'Got to buy the

ingredients for the carrot cake. Gonna bake it tonight. I don't want Granny Jackson on my bones.'

'No,' I replied. 'You certainly don't want Granny Jackson on your case. Don't tell Liccle Bit I said so, but she can be fierce!'

We said our goodbyes and Bossi followed me up the Falcon Ridge path. The higher we climbed, the colder it felt.

I've got a girlfriend. Shall I give her a call? No, too early. You just said to Jonah not to behave like a hound. I hope Wendy doesn't drag me on shopping missions to Crongton Broadway. I wonder if I should show her my garden and golf course designs? Is that a bit geeky? I wonder what her friends will make of me? I've only met Julie who attends the same school as Wendy. My attention span wanted to jet away after listening to all her Taylor Swift chat.

I made it to the top of Falcon Ridge. The breeze was stronger here. The pine trees swayed around us. It was very quiet. No birds chirped in the treetops. I climbed the four steps leading to the viewing platform. A waist-high stone wall encircled it. If offered a mega view of Shrublands, Spenge, Biggin Spires, Nobbler Fields and Corkscrew Spa. Juniper promised to hang-glide off here one day.

Dad used to take me up here as a kid and tell me the world could be mine if I worked hard enough.

'Yes, Colin. You get out of life what you put in. Always remember that.'

I wondered if Wendy and I would live in one of them towns when we were older. We'd have to have a big garden

Awaiting Punishment

for her horses. I'd build a maze for my friends to get lost in. I'd have an office where I'd do my golf course designing.

What am I saying? You haven't even been on a first date with her and you're thinking about living together. Just enjoy Boxing Day... if my parents don't have me on lockdown in the basement.

Before I left the viewing platform, I imagined designing a golf course where pine trees lined fairways and putting surfaces were backdropped by evergreens. I made a note on my phone.

I reached home just after 9.15 a.m.

Oh no!

Dad's dark green Range Rover was parked outside our front door.

They must've driven through the night. They were supposed to land here at lunchtime! Shall I go around the back, sneak in and make my way to my bedroom? And keep quiet for the rest of the day? No, that's lame. Let's get this over and done with. It's Christmas Eve. Maybe my punishment won't be so bad. They might've bought me a boring souvenir from the Highlands. A stupid mug with my name on it, or tartan socks or something. Just be polite and grateful, then I might get away with everything.

I entered the house. I looked to my right. My parents sat on stools in the kitchen. Mum sipped her green tea. She side-eyed me. Dad held his *To Kill a Mockingbird* mug of coffee. I could sniff its strength from where I stood. He munched on one of Maria's homemade ginger cookies. Bossi barked. There was no sign of Maria.

This could be bad.

For a moment there was silence. I unclipped Bossi's lead, and he went downstairs. Even he didn't want to hear what was about to be said.

'Have you got something you want to tell us?' asked Dad.

'Er . . . yeah, I had a party,' I admitted. 'It's no biggie.'

I scratched behind my ear.

'Why didn't you tell us you were planning something?' asked Mum.

'Cos, I didn't know till after you left,' I replied. 'It was a spur-of-the-moment kinda thing.'

'We could have organised it properly,' said Mum. 'I could have got someone in to cook a nice dinner. Your friends could've sat around the table. It would have been nice to meet them.'

'My school friend McKay baked some treats,' I said. 'He's a top-ranking chef. Or he's gonna be one day. Everyone loved his chicken rolls, patties and mince pies. I didn't want no big dinner kinda thing. There're still some mince pies left if *you* want any.'

'Your friends,' Dad said. He took a sip of his coffee and locked me in a hard stare. 'They ran amok in Mrs Smythe-Watson's front garden with Bossi. It scared the life out of her.'

'I never invited those guys!' I protested. 'They were gatecrashers.'

'You hosted the party,' Dad said. 'So you have to take responsibility.'

Awaiting Punishment

'You're not listening to me,' I argued. 'I DID NOT INVITE THEM! So how can they be *my* responsibility?'

'Would they have turned up if you hadn't had a party?' Mum asked.

'Er . . . probably not. But that's not the point. I didn't even give them my address. Someone leaked it to them.'

'Mrs Smythe-Watson is very shaken up,' Dad said.

'She'd be shaken up if a butterfly landed on her doorstep.'

'Don't be flippant, Colin!' Mum told me off.

'If you're planning to host anything again,' Dad said, 'please let us know. Some of our friends have kids the same age as you. They'd be interested in meeting you.'

'Let you know?' I repeated. 'I'm tired of meeting your friends' kids. They're proper boring. I don't wanna hear about their sailing holidays, their trips to watch the Monaco Grand Prix and their uncles who live in mega bungalows in Palm Springs.'

'You're exaggerating, Colin,' Dad said.

'And you're not really interested in anything I do,' I cut in. 'You're always jetting off to this cause or that, leaving me on my lonesome. You're more interested in grimy lakes and animals than me. On my last birthday, you didn't get home till after eleven. You said you had to attend some boring council meeting. It was Maria's day off, but she spent the evening with me watching a film.'

'They were planning to put up one of them tall pylons on Shrublands Road,' Dad explained. 'We must protect the natural beauty of our environment.'

'Yep, and that's more important than me.'

'That's unfair, Colin,' Mum said. 'We've given you a nice life. You can have anything you ask for.'

'Except having my parents around.'

Mum's gaze dropped to the floor. She placed a palm on her forehead. She then took her glasses off and wiped the lenses. I knew that comment wounded her.

It had to be said.

Dad lipped his coffee again. I had the urge to snatch his *To Kill a Mockingbird* mug and smash it to pieces. He took another bite of his biscuit. His eyes didn't leave me.

'We've worked hard for what we have,' he said. 'We didn't start with much. Just two university kids who came from working-class backgrounds. We wanted to make a mark in the world.'

I took a deep breath.

'Why did you decide to have a kid?' I asked.

Just then, Maria came downstairs. My parents swapped glances as Maria boiled the kettle and made herself a mint tea. She dropped a dose of honey into it. She grabbed a mince pie from the biscuit tin. I think she sensed the frost between my parents and me. 'Sorry,' she said. 'Didn't mean to intrude.' She carried her mug upstairs.

'Why did you have me?' I repeated the question. 'If you knew you wouldn't have time to look after me?'

'We love each other,' replied Mum. 'Yes, we had busy lives. When you were born, it made us very happy. We felt . . . complete.'

Awaiting Punishment

'Complete! I'm not a *James Bond* DVD collection! If I made you soooo happy, why was I looked after by so many babysitters when I was little? I don't remember you being there when I finished junior school for the day. It was always someone else making my tea or dinner. Do you have any idea what it was like to be just, what, six years old, being picked up from school by strangers every day? And watching TV on your own night after night? I guess you were busy making your mark in the world.'

'Colin!' Mum raised her voice. 'That's not called for.'

'We have good careers because of the study and work we put in,' said Dad. 'Something that we want you to develop – a strong work ethic. You get out what you put in.'

'Careers!' I interrupted. 'You and your careers! Dad, you've spent more time with some of your famous clients than you ever did with me. A babysitter taught me how to ride my first bike! I can't even remember her name. You sent another one to watch me doing the sack race on sports day when I was seven! I stopped telling my friends that sometimes you're on the news with whatever celebrity. It was like . . . it was like you were a stranger.'

'Finding a balance hasn't been easy,' said Mum. 'We tried our best.'

'Your best?' I repeated. 'You're a so-called psychiatrist, right? Didn't you ever think about how I was feeling being stuck here on my own? Yeah, I had babysitters who done stuff for me. But it's not the same.'

Silence.

Oh, my daisies. Look at their faces. Dad's brewing. Mum will start crying lakes soon. Did I go too far? No, I didn't. I can't stop now.

'Ground me if you want for the party,' I said. 'I don't *care*. I'm going to my room.'

'Colin!' Mum called.

I bounced up the stairs and didn't look back. I reached my room and slammed the door behind me.

For half an hour, I lay on my back and stared at the ceiling.

Am I spoilt? My friends don't have what I have. They'd kill for a pool table, a cinema-size TV screen and a back garden big enough for a horse to be happy in. But at least their parents are there for them.

I decided to get up and switch on my laptop. I watched a wildlife programme on Netflix about a mother cheetah raising her cubs in the African wild. I was getting into it when I heard a knock on my door.

28

Deception

'Come in,' I said.

Mum poked her head around my door. 'Your father wants you,' she said. 'He's in the garage.'

Blistering buttercups! I forgot to polish the DB5! He's seen the scratch.

'Er . . . what does he want?' I asked.

'Erm . . . I think he wants to ask you about the car.'

'Oh,' I said.

I switched off my laptop and slowly made my way to the garage.

How am I gonna explain this?

Dad had changed into his jeans and his brown woolly pullover. He held a broken padlock in his left hand. He studied the bonnet of the DB5 like he was in a science lab examining a deadly virus.

'A good try,' he said. 'I'll give you that. Is this your handiwork?'

'No,' I replied. 'It was my friend Liccle Bit.'

'Liccle Bit?' Dad repeated.

'His real name is Lemar. We call him Liccle Bit. He's short.'

'Of course. I must get this done professionally,' Dad said, his eyes still scanning the car's bodywork.

'You can hardly tell the difference,' I replied.

'But *I* can. I can see the scratch. It's quite deep. Whoever did it has a vicious streak.'

'It wasn't me.'

'But you tried to hide it from me.' Dad raised his voice. 'Haven't I said to not let anyone in the garage? Do you know how much this car costs me?'

'I didn't let anyone inside here,' I protested. 'They broke in.'

'Who?' Dad asked.

'The gatecrashers to my party.'

Dad stood up and shook his head. I sensed the disappointment in his eyes. 'That's convenient,' he said. 'Blame someone else.'

'It's true!' I shouted. 'Do you think I did it on purpose?'

'I don't know what to think.'

'Are you calling me a liar?'

'You should have told me about this when I was in the kitchen,' Dad said. 'Did I have to find out this way?'

'I still think Liccle Bit done a top-ranking job,' I said. 'You should be happy that we tried our best to repair it.'

Deception

'But you tried to deceive me.'

'Only cos I knew you would go nuclear with your reaction,' I argued. 'Even your car is more important than me.'

'That's not fair, Colin.'

'YES IT IS! You spend more time with it than you do with me. You spent all your summer holiday replacing the engine and other parts. Mum and I only saw you at dinner time.'

Dad took a few breaths. He placed his hands on his hips and stared at the floor. He eventually looked up.

'Let's calm down, shall we,' he said.

'I will, if you will,' I replied.

'There's something I'd like to discuss with you and your mum in my office,' he said.

'Oh? What's that?'

'You will find out soon enough.'

'Why not tell me now?'

'Because I want your mother to be present,' Dad explained. 'We like to make family decisions with everyone there to hear it.'

'Family decisions?' I repeated.

It sounded like he was chatting to a jury. *I'm his son!* Family bloody decisions. *He* made most of them. Mum and I hardly had a say.

Same old, same old. Maybe I should bounce up to my bedroom again and lock myself in. No, tired of that. Gonna stand up to him.

*

A Crongton Christmas Party

Five minutes later, I was parked in Dad's office in one of his black leather swivel chairs. Mum sat next to me. Framed photographs of vintage cars and film stars hung on the walls. My fave one was a black-and-white portrait of Boris Karloff with his square head as Frankenstein's monster. Creepy. There were others of Steve McQueen, Leslie Caron, James Dean, James Cagney, Humphrey Bogart, Mae West and a Volkswagen Beetle called Herbie. I'd never seen any of their old-school films. Shelves filled with legal files and books occupied the wall behind Dad's chair.

Propped up on his shiny wooden desk were photographs of Dad's parents and my uncle Stuart. For some reason, Dad didn't like me calling him Stuey. When I was little, he'd take me out to Crongton Heath to play football, rugby and cricket. I wasn't much good at any sport, but he taught me how to fly a kite. He moved to New Zealand when I was nine. Dad was very upset about it. He teaches PE at a school in Auckland. Stuey never forgets to send me birthday cards.

There was also a black-and-white pic of Gregory Peck on the desk in Dad's fave film: *To Kill a Mockingbird*. He watched it at least twice a year for inspiration.

His golf clubs were in a corner. I decided to rest my gaze on them.

'Mum and I've been thinking,' Dad began. 'That maybe a change of environment might do you some good.'

'What do you mean?' I asked. 'Are you thinking of moving?'

My parents swapped a glance. Mum fidgeted in her seat.

Deception

'Not quite,' Mum said. 'We just think that you should be exposed to more opportunities.'

'What do you mean opportunities?' I asked. 'Can you get to the point?'

'We originally sent you to South Crongton High so you could integrate in the local community,' Dad explained. 'To learn that for many, life isn't easy. Only interaction with, er, less fortunate kids can help achieve that. We wanted you to learn empathy with those not so lucky in life.'

'Attending a comprehensive school didn't do us any harm,' added Mum.

'But now,' Dad cut in, 'we feel we don't want you to miss opportunities because of the school you attend.'

'What are you saying?' I asked.

'I know the principal of Trinity Whitgift,' said Dad. 'We could get you registered there in time for the summer term.'

Did I hear right? Trinity Whitgift! Rich folks pay well over thirty-five grand a year for their kids to roll there. And I'd have to take a bus. It's near Biggin Spires. I only know one guy who attends that school: Clement Stevens. He spends his Saturday mornings mountain climbing and abseiling with his pops. He looks at me like something he picked up on his shoe from a dog park.

I didn't know what to say. I thought I was gonna be grounded.

That would've been better than this tragedy. What about my friends? When would I see them? I'd fade out of their lives. They'd stop visiting me. I'll be on my lonesome again.

'I've got some proper friends at South Crong High,' I said. 'They look out for me. They'd do anything for me.'

'Can they help you get a career?' Mum asked. 'Or give you a good connection?'

'I know what I want to do!' I insisted.

'Gardening can be a nice hobby,' Dad said. 'Something to do at weekends or during the summer holidays.'

'I want to be a landscape gardener,' I corrected.

'If you attend Trinity Whitgift, I'm sure you'll be inspired by something else,' Dad insisted. 'You'll have aspirational people all around you.'

'What's that supposed to mean?' I asked. 'I've got good friends around me. They're ambitious too. They've got my back, and I have theirs. I don't want to lose that.'

'I thought you mentioned that you get bullied at South Crongton?' Dad said.

'Yeah . . . well. Not as much as in Year Seven.'

'The headteacher, Mr Whittaker, said he'd make an appointment in the new year to see us. He'll give us a tour. The grounds and facilities they have at Trinity Whitgift are very impressive. They'll bring out all your potential.'

'I'm not going to Trinity Whitgift,' I protested. 'Why are you dropping this on me right now? All because Bossi ran across Mrs Smythe-Watson's precious front lawn?'

'We want what's best for you, Colin,' Mum said.

'This is not best for me! I wanna see my mates every day.'

'You can still invite your old school friends over,' Dad said.

Deception

'Are you sure about that, Dad? They all live on South Crong estate. Next time, they might run across your roof, jack your golf clubs and drive your DB5 into Mrs Smythe-Watson's conservatory!'

'There's no need to be sarcastic, Colin,' Mum said. 'Give it some thought. You will make new friends.'

'No, I won't! Everyone already thinks I'm weird around here. They'll think the same at Trinity Whitgift.'

'There will be teachers and students there who can really help you,' added Dad. 'We still live in a world where sometimes it's important who you know, rather than what you know.'

'I like who I know,' I said. 'And that's my friends at school! I'm *not* going to Trinity Whitgift. End of.'

I stood up, glanced at the framed pic of Boris Karloff, and walked out. I made my way upstairs passing Maria going down. She didn't say anything, but she had compassion in her eyes.

I parked in the chair at my desk when I got to my bedroom.

How am I gonna tell my friends that I might be leaving South Crong High? I never had real mates until I met Venetia, Saira, Jonah, Juniper, Liccle Bit and McKay. Even Kiran Cassidy invited me to his New Year's Eve rave. It'll be unbearable at Trinity Whitgift. Why can't my parents see that? They don't care.

I received a text message from Juniper.

Hi, Boy from the Hills. How's your Christmas Eve going down? I'm stuck in the shop. I've just had a thief running out with a packet of chocolate biscuits. I couldn't be arsed to chase him. I'm on my lonesome cos dad had to go out and get some supplies. By the way, wicked party! It's a shame about Kiran's partner choices. Ah, well. You can't have it all.

My Christmas Eve is tragic. Dad noticed the scratch on the DB5. They wanna send me to another school.

What school?

Trinity Whitgift.

Juniper decided to call me.

'Trinity Whitgift!' she said. 'That school with the cloaks and weird hats and where kids wear black lace-up shoes?'

'Yep, by Biggin Spires. It's like Hogwarts without any magic or cool headteachers.'

'What you gonna do?'

'I don't know,' I replied. 'What can I do?'

'You don't wanna go, right?' Juniper asked. 'They play that funny game of hockey with sticks and nets.'

'Lacrosse,' I corrected her.

'Yep, you don't want to attend any school that plays lacrosse,' said Juniper. 'You have to show your parents that you're serious about not attending.'

'How do I do that?' I asked. 'They don't care what I think. They want to do what they think is *best* for me.'

'You've got to think of something drastic,' Juniper advised. 'Once, in Year Seven, my parents believed a teacher

Deception

who claimed I started a fight. I couldn't believe it. I didn't start it, and I refused to chat to my folks for a week. It drove my pops kerbonkers. They had to take me seriously.'

'I don't think they'd take any notice if I stopped chatting to them,' I said.

'Whatever you decide,' Juniper added, 'make sure it gets their attention.'

'I won't fit in at Trinity Whitgift,' I said. 'No one there is gonna like me. It was bad enough when I first started at South Crong High.'

'Sometimes you do go on strange,' said Juniper. 'But we don't care. Hey, peeps at school call me a freak. We've all got a bit of weirdness in us. You're one of us now. A Crongton Knight. Remember that.'

'Thanks for saying. Hope it stays that way.'

'It will. Just remember, you gotta do something dramatic to show them you're not playing. Hold on a sec, I've got a customer. Somebody wants to charge their electric key.'

'Er . . . OK. Chat to you—'

Juniper killed the call.

Do something dramatic. What could that be?

29

The Great Escape

An hour later, I was working on my new golf course design when someone slapped my door. I didn't answer.

'It's me, Maria.'

'OK, come in.'

'Are you coming down for lunch?' Maria asked.

'Er . . . not hungry,' I replied.

'I made some fish fritters, fried plantain and tomato-mushroom omelette. It's very good, if I say so myself.'

'Where's my parents?' I asked.

'They've gone out to do some last-minute Christmas shopping,' Maria said.

'OK, I'll come down in a minute.'

Ten minutes later, I was sampling Maria's fish fritters, plantain and omelette. It had bits of pepper, onion

The Great Escape

and a dose of spice in it. McKay would've been impressed.

'Did you hear the breaking news?' I asked Maria.

Maria washed up a frying pan and a few plates in the sink. She didn't turn around.

'I said did you hear the breaking news?'

'I heard you the first time,' Mara replied. 'It's not my place to comment.'

'They're sending me to Trinity Whitgift.'

'Yes, I know.'

'My parents will probably go into town and ring the church bells for that one.'

Maria didn't smile at my joke.

'What should I do?'

Maria thought about it. She dried her hands with a paper towel before facing me.

'I see you're very close with your friends,' she said. 'That was obvious from your party. If it was me, I'd find it very difficult to start at a new school and leave good friends behind.'

'Mum and Dad don't get that,' I said. 'It's all careers and making the right connections for them. They don't care what I feel.'

'In their way, they're doing what they think is best for you.'

'Going to Trinity Whitgift is not best for me. It'll be a living nightmare.'

'Friends meant everything to me when I was at school,'

Maria added. 'Yes, those were the days. They end before you know it.'

'You don't think I should go, do you?'

'It's not for me to say,' Maria replied. 'All I can say is try to show them that friendships are just as important as career choices.'

'Don't know how I'm gonna do that.'

Maria patted me on the shoulder. 'It will all work out.'

'I hope it does.'

I returned to my room to work on a water feature for my golf course design – a bubbly stream flowing beneath a stone bridge. I thought about calling Wendy. She had to attend Joan Benson, a school she didn't love.

She once said that she doesn't complain about it too much cos she knows her parents worked hard to send her there. She might advise me to go to Trinity Whitgift. I don't want an argument with her before our first proper date. I decided not to ding her.

Maria cooked a lamb, carrot and onion casserole for dinner with boiled baby potatoes, roasted parsnips and red cabbage. During the meal, hardly anything was said. If a ladybird stepped across the dinner table, we all would've heard it. Everyone side-eyed each other. Mum did mention how she loved the scenery of the Highlands, the mystery of the deep lakes and the tasty salmon breakfast she had at the hotel, but I wasn't really listening. I thought on Juniper's words.

You gotta do something dramatic.

The Great Escape

Dad's eyes never left his plate. He sank a big glass of brandy and Coke with his dinner. Mum sipped her red wine. Maria and I drank Diet Coke.

Maria said she had baked rhubarb crumble for dessert. She offered to make some custard to go with it. It was my favourite, but I didn't stay for it. Instead, I took Bossi for his evening trod. It felt good to get out of the house. For a short moment, I did consider letting him loose in Mrs Smythe-Watson's back garden. That would teach the queen of snitches.

Halfway up the Falcon Ridge path, I decided what I had to do.

Yes, that'll get my parents' attention. They'll have to rethink the whole situation. Trinity Whitgift is not gonna see my ass!

I returned home just after seven-thirty. Mum was in the kitchen chatting on the phone. Pops worked in his office. I went upstairs to my room, switched on my laptop and watched three episodes of *Peaky Blinders*.

I heard someone climbing the stairs just after 10 p.m. They tapped my door.

'Come in,' I called.

Mum poked her head around the door. 'Goodnight,' she said. 'Think about what we spoke about. We only want the best for you. Don't worry about the car. Your dad will get over it.'

'He overreacted,' I said.

'You know what he's like with his toys.'

I nodded. 'Goodnight, Mum.'

Dad went to bed just before 11 p.m. He didn't say goodnight, but I heard him flush the toilet and brush his teeth.

I switched off my laptop. From the bottom of my wardrobe, I picked up my school shoulder bag. I emptied the books out of it and filled it with underwear and T-shirts. I squeezed in my black pullover too.

Boy from the Hills, this is drastic. Do you really want to do this? It'll get their attention. It might piss them off forever. I'll be grounded for eternity. But at least they'll think twice about sending me to Trinity Whitgift.

I slipped into my trainers and pulled on my fave green hoodie. Quietly, I made my way down the stairs. I heard the hum of the fridge. It always sounded louder at night-time. I headed for the kitchen where I grabbed two mince pies. I thought about taking a slice of Maria's rhubarb crumble.

No, I need to make my great escape.

I stepped towards the front door when I spotted Bossi at the top of the basement staircase. He wagged his tail.

'Bossi,' I whispered. 'I have to take this mission on my own. Maria will look after you.'

Bossi looked at me and trotted towards the front door. He barked and pricked his ears.

'Ssssshhhh! Bossi, I'm sorry. I can't take you with me.'

I opened the front door, checked the stairs and closed it carefully. I felt a dose of guilt for leaving Bossi behind. I hoped he wouldn't bounce upstairs and alert my parents that I had gone.

The Great Escape

You must do something dramatic. Juniper's words echoed in my head again.

It was a cold night. I munched one of the mince pies in two bites. The grass on the Heath had a frosty film on its surface. It felt crunchy to walk on. I checked behind me. No one followed. I glanced up to my parents' bedroom window. No light switched on. Relief.

Behind my house, the Crongton Hills and forest rose in dark shapes. The stars had come out to play. A quarter moon lit the north-east sky. If there really was a Santa, he and his reindeers would be freezing their butts off up there. I passed the Crongton Recreation Ground on my left and imagined Jonah and Merlene running around the track. Memories of Uncle Stuey flying a kite filled my head.

I wish he was here.

Fifteen minutes later, I entered the South Crongton estate. There weren't so many Christmas fairy lights nicing up folks' windows here. South Crong High looked proper spooky at night. My ears felt cold, so I pulled up my hoodie. There weren't too many folks about apart from the odd kerb rat whizzing by on their bike. Someone was singing along very badly to Wham's *Last Christmas* from a second-floor flat. I spotted a man sleeping in the back seat of a black Mini.

I reached my destination. Dickens House. Fifteen floors high. I checked the time. 11.40 p.m.

I hope he's still up.

I pulled out my phone and punched the number.

'McKay! Are you up?'

'Yeah,' McKay replied. 'I'm playing FIFA with Nesta on the PlayStation. Why are you dinging me so late?'

'I'm downstairs.'

'What do you mean you're downstairs.'

'That's what I mean,' I replied. 'I'm downstairs for real. Buzz me in.'

'It's . . . it's nearly midnight,' McKay said. 'It's Christmas Eve. Shouldn't you be laying out your stocking or giving Santa a glass of milk? Have you done something cadazy like run away?'

'Er . . . can you buzz me in? It's proper cold out here. The polar bears are wearing mittens.'

The door made an angry bee sound. I pulled it open and stepped into the lift. I pressed for the seventh floor. I sniffed something foul coming from a corner. I couldn't look at it.

McKay had already opened his front door. He stood on his welcome mat outside it. 'What's going on?' he asked. 'Your pops found out about the scratch on his precious?'

'Yeah, he did,' I replied. 'But it's not that.'

'Then what is it?'

I followed McKay into his flat. His brother, Nesta, was parked on the couch playing his football game on the TV. The peak of his FC Barcelona baseball cap pointed to his left. He raised a hand. 'What's going on, Boy from the Hills? Merry Christmas and all of that.'

'Merry Christmas to you too,' I replied.

The Great Escape

McKay headed for the kitchen. I sniffed something roasting in the cooker. 'I slapped the turkey in the oven about half an hour ago,' McKay explained. 'It's on a slow roast. I just want to concentrate on the veg tomorrow.'

'My parents are taking me out of school and sending me to Trinity Whitgift,' I blurted out.

'Trinity Whitgift!' McKay repeated. 'That's all the way near Biggin Spires. Are they serious?'

'Yep, they're double serious. I'm not going.'

'They start school at eight and don't finish till five,' McKay said. 'Then they've got the after-school clubs. They've got their own cricket ground, swimming pool *and* tennis courts.'

'I don't care what they've got,' I said. 'I'm not going.'

'Do . . . do your parents know you're out roaming on street?'

'Er . . . not exactly,' I replied.

'What do you mean, not exactly?' asked Nesta. He had paused his game, stepped to the kitchen and poured himself a glass of orange juice. His cap covered his eyebrows. He looked at me suspiciously. 'I hope you're not gonna bring any of your family drama to our gates,' he added.

'I snuck out,' I admitted. 'Can . . . can I stay the night?'

Nesta and McKay swapped a glance.

'I'll . . . I'll have to ask Dad,' said McKay. 'He's sleeping.'

'OK.' I nodded.

'Do you want a drink and a couple of fried dumplings?' McKay offered. 'I made them for lunch earlier.'

A Crongton Christmas Party

'Yeah,' I replied. 'I'll have an orange juice. Thanks.'

McKay warmed up two fried dumplings for me in the microwave and served my orange juice. 'I did make some ackee and saltfish to go with it,' he said. 'But Dad finished it before he went to sleep.'

'That's OK.'

'I'll ask Pops if it's all right if you can stay,' McKay said.

'Good luck with waking him,' Nesta said.

I sat on a stool in the kitchen. I sank my snack. Nesta resumed his football game.

What am I gonna do if McKay's dad doesn't let me stay? Maybe I could go to Liccle Bit's flat? No, his place is too crowded. Jonah? No, his place is like a warzone with his parents arguing all the time. Venetia? They're good Christians. They might let someone stay at their inn for the night. No, bad idea. Liccle Bit will get all jealous. And Venetia's little twin sisters scare the spine out of me.

McKay was gone for three minutes. It felt like three hours. My heart left-hooked my chest.

Mr Tambo was dressed in a string vest and black tracksuit bottoms. There was a hole in his left sock. His eyes were half-closed.

'McKay tells me you're having a little trouble at home,' Mr Tambo said.

'Er . . . yes. I just wanna stay the night.'

'On Christmas Eve?' Mr Tambo checked his watch. 'It must've been more than a little trouble.'

'I . . . I needed to get away,' I said. 'It . . . it was becoming a bit intense.'

The Great Escape

'And do your parents know where you are?' Mr Tambo asked. I felt the heat of his gaze. He crossed his arms.

'Er . . . not exactly,' I replied.

'You can stay as long as you tell them where you are,' Mr Tambo insisted.

'I'll . . . I'll call them in the morning.'

'They'll be worrying about you,' Mr Tambo said. 'Do you want them to fret all night?'

'If I tell them where I am now, they'll only come here and get me. And if they do, I won't be going home with them. Not tonight. I . . . I need the space to think.'

'You have put me in a very difficult position,' said Mr Tambo. He glanced at McKay.

'I'm very sorry,' I said. 'I don't want to cause any drama. Especially on Christmas Eve. If it's too much trouble, I'll go somewhere else.'

Somewhere else, Boy from the Hills? Are you kidding yourself?

I pulled out my phone. I checked my messages and missed calls. There was nothing. 'They don't even know I've gone,' I said.

Mr Tambo shook his head and placed his hands on his hips. He thought about something. 'I don't want you to go anywhere else,' he said. 'It's bad enough you walking the streets of South Crongton estate at this time of night. It's not all joy to all men out there.'

'So, can I stay?' I asked.

Mr Tambo exchanged glances with McKay. Nesta paused his game. I don't know why I didn't notice it before, but a small silver Christmas tree blinked with fairy lights in a corner.

'You can stay on one condition,' Mr Tambo said. 'You call your parents first thing in the morning. And when I say first thing, I don't mean at eleven o'clock.'

'Yes.' I nodded. 'Definitely. Thanks very much.'

'And if you don't, I'll call them myself,' Mr Tambo added. He turned to McKay. 'Isn't there a spare pillow and duvet cover in your wardrobe?'

'Yes.' McKay nodded. 'Remember, I've got to get up early in the morning and deliver my carrot cake. Granny Jackson is expecting it. Boy from the Hills can come with me.'

'Not before he calls his parents,' Mr Tambo replied, then yawned and stretched out his arms. Every time I see him, he's always tired. 'Now,' he said. 'If there isn't anything else, I'm going back to my bed.'

'Goodnight, Dad.'

'Sleep good, Dad.'

'Goodnight, Mr Tambo. Thanks for letting me stay over.'

McKay went to collect my bedding. Nesta stopped his game and switched off the TV. 'I'll play this on the smaller screen in my room,' he said. 'Before you go to sleep, make sure you switch off all the lights.'

'Yeah, of course,' I replied.

Nesta stepped to his room. McKay returned with my duvet and pillow. 'The last time I had a sleepover here, I caught Liccle Bit sampling my prawn cocktail crisps in the middle of the night.'

The Great Escape

I laughed. 'How old were you?'

'Eight, I think,' McKay replied. 'Mum made meatballs, garlic bread and spaghetti with her special sauce.'

'I'm sure it was delici-ocious.'

'It was,' said McKay. 'How did your pops react when he spotted the scratch on his precious?'

'He was sort of . . . calm,' I replied. 'But calm with him is not good. I'd prefer him to shout and scream and get it over with. I still think Liccle Bit did a top-ranking job.'

'He did,' agreed McKay. 'Your dad could work for the feds forensics team with his eagle eyes.'

'He's gonna get it done professionally,' I said.

'Don't have to pay for it, do you?'

'Nope. My pocket money could never cover it.'

'That's a relief. Those professional peeps charge nuff dollars.'

'How did it go with Ava?' I asked.

McKay grinned. 'All good, all good. She had a bubbling time at your party. She wants to go to Kiran Cassidy's New Year's Eve rave.'

'You guys going on a date during the holidays?'

'I'm working on it,' replied McKay. 'Let's see how we roll at Kiran's ting and I'll take it from there. How about you and Wendy?'

'I'm going to the races with her on Boxing Day. I have to get up at stupid o'clock. She's got a horse called Captain Heath running over the hurdles.'

'She loves her horses, right?'

'Yep, she's gonna be a jockey.'

'It's cadazy, isn't it,' McKay said. 'One minute, it's only Liccle Bit dating Venetia. Now, you're going out with Wendy. Ava's coming with me to Kiran's New Year's Eve rave, and Jonah's trying to get to first base with Shira.'

'Is she coming?'

McKay shook his head. 'I gave him Shira's phone number. Jonah said he was gonna ding her, but I haven't heard anything since. He might have got a big, fat blank . . . Don't say anything to him.'

'I won't,' I promised.

'Anyway,' McKay said. 'I've got a busy day tomorrow. I have to drop off the carrot cake, then come back and steam and roast the veg. I have to make the spicy gravy too. And the stuffing. We sit down for dinner right after the King's speech. That's how Mum used to do it.'

'Must be hard,' I said. 'Christmas time . . . you know . . . with your mum not here.'

'It is,' replied McKay. 'Last year we didn't really do anything. Just sat around feeling sorry for ourselves. Nesta went out on his bike at lunchtime. We didn't see him again till Boxing Day morning. Dad . . . Dad had a hard time that day.'

He stared into space. I decided to change the subject.

'All right,' I said. 'Thanks for letting me stay. I'll call my folks tomorrow, but no matter what they say, I'm not going to Trinity Whitgift.'

McKay went to his room. I moved to the couch where I pulled off my trainers and hoodie. I made myself comfortable before covering myself with the duvet. I wondered if my parents had fallen asleep yet. I checked my phone. Still no missed calls or messages from them. I stared at it for a while. Then I decided to switch it off.

30

Three Meals a Day

I struggled to catch sleep. I kept on sitting up and checking the front door. I don't know why, but I imagined my parents breaking in and dragging me off to Trinity Whitgift. I got up at 2.30 a.m. to stretch my legs and look out the window. I sank a glass of water. It suddenly hit me that I had never spent a Christmas Eve night away from home.

I picked up my phone and was about to switch it on.

You got to do something dramatic. Juniper's words repeated in my head.

Boy from the Hills, go and lie down. You might as well get some rest, whatever happens, you're in mega-trouble anyways.

I went back to the sofa. I tossed and turned. Minutes seemed to turn into hours.

*

I must have fallen asleep cos I sniffed something in the air. I sat up, wiped my eyes and heard McKay whistling. He was cooking something in a large frying pan.

'What . . . what's the time?' I asked.

'Just after seven,' McKay replied. 'I've got some chicken sausages and bacon in the oven. I'm frying some plantain, tomatoes and scrambling eggs. Is that all good for you?'

'Yeah, of course. Thanks.'

'All part of the service. The turkey's looking sweet and golden brown. I took it out half an hour ago. Nice and moist.'

McKay went back to his whistling. 'What do you drink in the morning?' he asked.

'Er . . . a hot chocolate will be good.'

McKay pointed at the kettle. 'Chocolate is in the cupboard, milk in the fridge. Make yourself useful.'

I made myself a drink. I had four sips before McKay served me my breakfast. 'Nesta and your dad still sleeping?'

'Yeah,' McKay replied. 'They won't get up until around ten. Maybe eleven. I've always been an early bird. My mum was the same way. Are you gonna ding your parents?'

'Er . . . yeah . . . As soon as I have my breakfast.'

I felt a big boot of guilt. *They must have checked my bedroom by now and realised I'm not at home.*

What will they do? They might think I got up early to take Bossi for his walk. But I left Bossi behind. Juniper's not wrong. It's gonna be dramatic.

'I'm gonna take my shower,' McKay said. 'Then I'll have my breakfast, clean up a bit, then we'll step to Liccle Bit's slab.'

'That's all good with me.' I nodded.

McKay's breakfast was good. Especially the plantain. Neat and sweet. My phone felt heavy in my pocket. My head told me to drop my pride and call my parents. My stubborn ego didn't allow me to do that.

They must've discovered that I'm not at home. They'll interrogate Maria. Dad will have to take Bossi for his walk. Mum will probably call Wendy. A good thing my parents don't have the rest of my friends' phone numbers.

Fifteen minutes later, McKay came out of his room dressed in a Christmas sweater and black jeans.

'You call them?' he asked.

'Er . . . yeah, but it went to voicemail,' I lied. 'They had a long drive yesterday. They're probably catching up on some sleep.'

'Did you tell them where you are?'

'Er, yeah.'

'So, are you going back home today?'

'Later,' I replied. 'Not yet. I said I'm going to Liccle Bit's flat and then on to the community centre. They're good with that.'

I felt bad for lying to McKay.

I just can't face dinging my parents right now. Dad will go off on one of his lectures and Mum will start crying. Can't deal with that right now.

Three Meals a Day

McKay sank his breakfast as I had my shower. He had given me a spare flannel and towel. When I changed into my clothes, I once again thought about calling my folks.

Not yet. But maybe you should ding Wendy. But I can't call her in front of McKay.

I helped McKay peel and slice Brussels sprouts, carrots, cabbage and potatoes before we left for Liccle Bit's slab. He carried his foil-wrapped carrot cake in a plastic bag.

'Venetia's mum made a fruit trifle,' McKay said. 'She's meeting us at the community centre at ten. Juniper's bringing a few packets of chocolate biscuits and a chocolate log from her store. Jonah texted me earlier. He's picking up something from his uncle in Ashburton.'

'What kinda folks go to the Crongton soup kitchen on Christmas Day?' I asked.

'Anyone,' McKay replied. 'You don't have to be in Team Jesus to get a meal.'

As we stepped across the green to Liccle Bit's block, I felt good that I was with a friend on Christmas Day.

Liccle Bit answered the door.

'Merry Christmas!' I greeted.

Liccle Bit's eyes went all round and big. 'Kiss Santa's black boots!' he said. 'You ran away from home!'

'Ssssshhhhh!' I replied. 'It's not a biggie. I'll be going home later. By the way, how do you know?'

'McKay texted me late last night,' Liccle Bit replied. 'Everyone knows.'

'Er . . . what do you mean everyone?' I asked.

'Venetia, Juniper, Saira and Jonah. Saira said not to phone-bomb you, but I know Jonah tried to ding you.'

'Er . . . my phone needs juice.'

Liccle Bit led us into his flat. His teen-cave was the box room on the left of the hallway. Granny Jackson was in the kitchen peeling sweet potatoes. She rocked a red, gold and green headscarf, a pink dressing gown and rabbit-face slippers. The smell of turkey smacked my nostrils. 'Merry Christmas!' she greeted. 'Colin? Is it? And McKay. And is that what me think it is you're carrying?'

'Yes.' McKay nodded. 'Carrot cake. My best yet.'

'Did you put the nutmeg and cinnamon in it?'

'I sure did,' replied McKay. 'And the raisins.'

'Excellent! Me shoulda ask you to make one for myself.'

'Maybe next time,' McKay said.

'I'll be bringing my rum cake,' Granny Jackson said. 'Me hope me never put too much white rum in it. Me don't want the good people of Crongton to walk out of the soup kitchen all drunk-up.'

McKay and I laughed.

Granny Jackson turned to me. 'Colin. Me don't think me ever see you on Christmas Day. Are your parents away? You staying wid McKay for the Christmas?'

'Er . . . no,' I replied. 'Just helping out McKay this morning.'

'Yes,' McKay said. 'He's my elf for the day.'

Granny Jackson wasn't convinced. 'What are your parents cooking today?' she asked. 'Turkey wid all of the trimmings?'

'Er . . . yes, I think so. Last year we had goose. I didn't really like it. The year before we had a capon.'

'What's a capon?' Liccle Bit asked.

'A big, fat man-chicken,' replied McKay.

'Where's your mum and Elaine?' I asked, wanting to change the subject.

'Still sleeping,' replied Liccle Bit. 'They were doing stuff in the kitchen late last night while I was babysitting Jerome. He didn't go to sleep till after two.'

'Me going to make myself presentable,' Granny Jackson said. 'Soon come. Wait in the front room for me.'

We did as we were told.

Family portraits sketched by Liccle Bit hung from the walls. There was even one of little Jerome. I wondered if Manjaro, the king G of South Crong – and Jerome's dad – had any role in his life.

I dare not ask.

A metre-high Christmas tree stood in the corner. The angel on top of it had a lopsided face. Red and silver tinsel decorated the door frames and around the TV.

'So, your pops didn't love my artwork?' Liccle Bit asked.

'Nope,' I replied.

'Liberties!' Liccle Bit said. 'My colours were on point.'

'My dad would have noticed if an invisible virus had coughed on his DB5,' I explained. 'He's forensic when it comes to his precious ride. It's all he cares about.'

'Did he kick off?' asked Liccle Bit.

'Not so much,' I said. 'But my folks want to send me to Trinity Whitgift.'

'Yeah, I heard.' Liccle Bit shook his head. 'And that's why you made your great escape?'

'Obviously.'

'I ran away once,' Liccle Bit admitted. 'When I got home, it wasn't my parents who gave me a beatdown, it was Elaine. I've still got the bruises.'

McKay and I laughed.

'Are you coming to the soup kitchen?' I asked.

'Yeah.' Liccle Bit nodded. He spoke in a whisper. 'If I stay here, I'll be on peeling veg duty. Or some other chore.'

Fifteen minutes later, Granny Jackson appeared in a red dress, white shoes and black beads in her grey hair. She wore a thick, pink scarf that was long enough to lap around a running track.

'You boys ready?' she asked.

'Yes, we are,' said McKay.

Liccle Bit led us out of the flat. It was nearly ten o'clock. My parents must've discovered by now that I wasn't at home. My phone felt as heavy as a brick.

'Come walk wid me, Colin,' Granny Jackson said. 'Tell me about how your family is celebrating Christmas. It was good to see you in church the other day.'

'Er . . . we don't do too much,' I replied. 'My folks just came back from Scotland. They're tired.'

Granny Jackson locked me in her gaze. Suddenly, my

head heated up. My forehead felt like it was dissolving. I could no longer pretend that everything was all good back at my gates.

'Everyting all right, Colin?' Granny Jackson asked. 'You don't look too well.'

'I . . . I didn't sleep too good last night.'

'You want a sip of water? Me have a bottle in me bag.'

'No, no. I'm all right.'

Granny Jackson pulled my arm and stood in front of me. McKay and Liccle Bit walked ahead of us.

'Are you sure everyting is all right at home?' Granny Jackson asked. She searched my eyes.

I tried my best not to cry.

Boy from the Hills! Stop being pathetic.

'Er . . . not exactly,' I admitted.

'What happened?' she asked.

I took in a deep breath. McKay and Liccle Bit didn't even notice that we were no longer with them.

'My parents don't get it,' I said.

I spilled everything to Granny Jackson, including the party, Vincent Chapman and Donald Thompson, what happened to Dad's DB5 and my folks wanting to send me to Trinity Whitgift. She nodded and narrowed her eyes. She *ummed* and *ahhhhed*. As I came to the end of my tale, the community centre was in sight. I couldn't see McKay and Liccle Bit.

They must have gone inside.

'Here's what you must do,' instructed Granny Jackson.

'You must call your parents quick-time. Tell them where you are.'

'But, but . . .'

'No buts. Call them now! They must be fretting. When you finish the call, come inside the community centre and help out.'

'OK,' I agreed.

I waited until Granny Jackson entered the community centre before I pulled out my phone and switched it on. I had fifteen missed calls. Seven were from Mum, four from Dad, two from Wendy and two from Jonah. I also had thirty-eight WhatsApp messages. One was from Uncle Stuey.

I'll answer them later.

I sucked in a mighty breath and called Mum.

'Colin! We've been worried sick! Where the hell are you? Are you OK?'

'Yes, I'm OK, Mum.'

'Why did you take off like that? What time did you leave the house?'

'Mum, please don't go off on one. I'm OK. I . . . I just needed space to think.'

'Where are you?'

'I'm at the Crongton Community Centre. The Crongton soup kitchen have set up here. They're gonna be serving free hot meals from twelve o'clock.'

'We'll come and get you,' Mum said.

'You can if you want, but I'm *not* going to Trinity Whitgift.'

'We can talk about that later!' Dad said. I was clearly on speakerphone. He didn't sound too happy. 'The important thing is that you're safe. Maria knocked on your door about six. Bossi was agitated about something. We thought he wanted to go out for a walk.'

'And it was a shock to discover you weren't there,' added Mum. 'We called Wendy, and she told us that she had no idea where you were.'

'Don't you and Dad stress her. She didn't know a thing.'

'Please don't do anything like that ever again,' said Mum. 'I was going to call the police.'

'Where have you been?' asked Dad.

'I went to McKay's.'

'McKay's?'

'A school friend. He baked all the snacks for my party. His dad let me stay over. He cooked me a nice breakfast this morning.'

'We're coming to get you,' insisted Mum.

'No need to rush,' I said. 'I'm gonna help out a bit at the community centre. And when you come, don't make a scene.'

'Are you sure you're all right?' Mum asked again.

'I'm all good, Mum. I just want you guys to listen to what I want, rather than decide for me.'

'Stay where you are,' instructed Mum. 'We'll be there in the next half an hour.'

'OK,' I said. 'But as I said, I'm gonna help out here for a little while.'

A Crongton Christmas Party

I killed the call.

That wasn't so bad.

I closed my eyes, sucked in a few breaths and made my way to the community centre.

Long tables were covered with paper tablecloths. A woman wearing a hijab laid out knives, forks and spoons. Tiny green Christmas trees stood at each place alongside a cracker. Paper chains helped hide the peeling ceiling. Cardboard cutouts of Santas and Christmas trees were Blu-Tacked to the walls. At the end of the hall was a kitchen. It had a sliding hatchway. Christmas songs played from an old-school radio.

I recognised the Reid brothers – Desmond and Clifton. They supervised the cooking and the volunteers. Granny Jackson, Liccle Bit and McKay were with them. It looked like they had received instructions. I headed towards the counter.

'We're on carving duty,' said McKay. 'There are four big turkeys to slice on four tables under the sign Cratchit's Corner. We must put on hygienic gloves and face masks. Don't want anyone sneezing on the food.'

'OK.' I nodded. 'No problem.'

After we had put on our protection, Desmond and Clifton led McKay and me to the tables where four mega turkeys rested on oval-shaped silver trays. We were both handed a large fork and a carving knife.

'Thanks so much for helping out,' Desmond said. 'Two volunteers went down sick last night.'

Desmond stepped to Granny Jackson, who was on rice duty.

'I can only do this for an hour,' McKay said. 'Then I've got to hot-toe to my castle and start the veg.'

We started carving.

Through the hatchway, I spotted early-comers taking their seats. Everyone said merry Christmas to each other. I can't lie, I felt a buzz of goodness doing something nice for the community.

Fifteen minutes later, Venetia entered with her fruit and custard trifle, Saira carried a velvet cake and Juniper brought in a few packets of chocolate biscuits and a long chocolate log. A table was prepped for all the sweet stuff. They came over to me and asked if I was OK.

'He's all good,' said McKay. 'I fed him well!'

'My parents are on their way,' I said. 'I hope they don't embarrass me.'

'They won't,' said Saira. 'Not here.'

'You would've made more of an impact if you ran away to the hills,' said Juniper. 'And stayed there for a week . . . or two. I've got a tent and sleeping bag you can borrow.'

'What would I live on?' I asked.

'You could come out during the night and raid peeps' bins,' replied Juniper. 'Trust me, after that, your parents will dare not even think about sending you to Trinity Whitgift.'

Everyone laughed.

A Crongton Christmas Party

Next to come through the entrance was Jonah. He brought with him a dozen Victoria sponge cupcakes. 'From my uncle,' he announced. 'And Boy from the Hills! Don't you answer your calls? I was proper worried about you.'

'I'm OK,' I said. 'I just needed . . . time.'

'I said not to call him,' snapped Saira. 'I guess we've all had times when we wanted to run away. I know I have.'

Everyone nodded.

'Can one of you take over from me?' asked McKay. 'I've got to get back to my castle and put on the veg.'

'Yes, I'll do it,' replied Saira.

'You have to put on gloves and a face mask,' I advised. 'And don't sneeze. Welcome to Cratchit's Corner! Happy holidays. Thanks for everything.'

31

Family Reunion

Two minutes later, I spotted someone else enter the building. For a short second my blood stopped flowing. Mum hot-stepped into the hall. She looked here and there. She was followed by Dad, who scanned the chairs and tables.

'Over here, Mum,' I called out.

She waved and smiled at me before her expression switched. As she approached me, I thought she might beat me down like Chapman and Thompson. I stared at a turkey. I had carved one and was about to mutilate another.

Mum's tone changed again. She smiled awkwardly. Dad had finally caught up with her. He looked like he'd rather be playing golf.

'These are my school friends.' I began making introductions. 'McKay, Saira, Venetia, Liccle Bit, Jonah and Juniper.'

Mum shook their hands. 'Merry Christmas to everyone,' she managed. 'It's lovely to meet you.'

'Merry Christmas, Mr and Mrs Scott,' Venetia replied.

'Merry Christmas.'

Dad took in his surroundings. 'This . . . this is very impressive,' he said. 'Does it happen every year?'

'It started six years ago,' Venetia explained. 'It's for anybody who feels alone during the holidays.'

'Or hungry,' Juniper added.

'Who runs it?' Dad asked.

'The Reid brothers,' I said. I pointed out who they were. 'Desmond's in charge of the cooking and his brother, Clifton, deals with all the organising. Their mum started it, but she sadly passed away. Breast cancer.'

'I'm sorry to hear,' said Dad.

'Everyone was sorry. It's just got bigger and bigger.'

'And the local community all contributes?' Dad asked.

'Yep,' McKay said. 'Anyone who can, brings a little something. You can volunteer if you want to. It all helps. Peeps who come get as good a Christmas dinner and dessert as anyone else. There's even a veggie option.'

'I'm sorry,' Dad said. 'I wasn't aware of this. Maybe I should've been. Otherwise, we would've brought a contribution.'

'It's all right, Dad,' I said. 'Bring something next year.'

'We certainly will.' Mum nodded.

'How long will you be here?' asked Dad.

'Er . . . I'm not sure,' I replied.

Family Reunion

'You can go,' said Saira. 'I can take over the carving. Go on, Boy from the Hills. Spend time with your family.'

Everyone looked at me.

'Are you sure?' I asked.

'Double sure.' Jonah nodded. 'Haven't you got school issues to sort out? You know, get prepped in Trinity Whitgift uniform.'

'Jonah!' Venetia raised her voice.

'Just joking,' Jonah replied.

'Turkey's nearly ready,' Mum said. 'Veg is on the boil. Roast potatoes are done.'

'Before I go . . .' I locked my gaze on Dad. 'I don't have to go to Trinity Whitgift, do I?'

Everyone hushed. All eyes were lasering on my pops. He scratched his nose. He glanced at Crongton folk entering the hall and taking their seats. He side-eyed Desmond and Clifton supervising the cooking. He then smiled at my friends.

'You have good friends and connections all around you,' Dad said. 'Attending Trinity Whitgift can't improve on that.'

'Yeah!' yelled Juniper. 'No playing with sticks and funny nets for you!'

'Or having to dress in weird uniforms,' added Jonah.

'And black lace-up shoes,' added Juniper.

Dad grinned away his embarrassment.

My smile stretched wider than Crongton Heath. Relief flooded my arteries.

Mum led me out of the centre. 'Your Christmas present is in your room,' she said.

'Did you get Maria something?' I asked.

I better get her something too. Even if I give it to her on Boxing Day.

'Of course.' Dad nodded. 'We know she gets lonely, so we offered to pay for return flights when she wants to visit her family.'

'That's generous,' I agreed. 'She really misses her folks and friends.'

'We know she does,' added Mum.

'Bossi will be glad to see you,' said Dad. 'He wouldn't go for a walk with me.'

'I'll take him for his trod when we get home,' I said. 'I'm gonna miss him.'

'Dinner will be ready when you're back.'

That nice warm feeling I had when I entered the centre returned. *My parents are mess-ups and far from perfect. But they're my mess-ups.* I grinned to myself. *They're a work-in-progress. I guess I'll have to teach them to do better. Ah, well. More homework.*

Epilogue

Maria cried oceans when I returned. I don't think it was cos of my family reunion. She was so excited about going home to see her family and friends. She gave me a long hug. My parents had also given her a month's holiday of her choosing.

Bossi nearly knocked me out with his greeting. He slobbered me like I was a piece of duck meat. My parents had bought me a bigger screen for my computer. It had fab picture quality and apps to help my landscape designing.

Christmas dinner included a mega-normous turkey, carrots, parsnips, stuffing, cabbage and a deep tray of macaroni cheese that Mum had baked. I sent a pic of it to McKay and he gave it top ratings.

I totally pigged out.

Dad served champagne to Maria and Mum, and I had to make do with this apple-cidery thing.

A Crongton Christmas Party

Uncle Stuey called just before six. It was the middle of the night in New Zealand, but he wanted to hear my voice. He asked me about my golf course designs and wondered when my parents would take me to visit him. Dad went all quiet.

'Auckland is beautiful,' he said. 'Right now, I'm taking a stroll around the harbour. When you visit, I'll take you out sailing on a yacht that a friend of mine owns.'

Later that evening, Wendy came around. She smuggled in half a bottle of red wine and paper cups. I tried it. Even with a dose of lemonade, I didn't like it too much. The apple-cidery thing was better.

'You drink this stuff?' I asked.

'Only on birthdays and at Christmas,' she replied. 'When is your birthday again?'

'The fourth of March,' I said.

'That's not too far away,' she replied. 'You should do something. Reaching fifteen is a biggie. Why don't you have a party?'

COOK LIKE THE SOUTH CRONG CREW

If you'd like to cook these delicious recipes, please take extra care and ask an adult to help if needed.

Maria's Fish Fritters

INGREDIENTS

350 g boneless saltfish cod
1 tsp baking powder
1 tsp chilli powder or hot pepper sauce
1 tbsp all-purpose seasoning
1 tsp freshly ground black pepper
2 tsp dried thyme
salt
300 g plain flour
1 medium onion, diced
1 Scotch bonnet pepper, deseeded and diced
2 garlic cloves, finely chopped
3 spring onions, sliced
2 small tomatoes, diced
Vegetable oil, for shallow frying

METHOD

Put the saltfish in a saucepan and cover with cold water. Bring to the boil and simmer for a few minutes. Add more water if necessary.

Remove the saltfish and use a fork to shred it, then place

into a mixing bowl. Add the baking powder and the rest of the dry ingredients apart from the flour. Next add the chilli. Then add 250 ml of cold water.

Add the flour and remaining ingredients and mix everything together. The mixture should be a thick, sloppy consistency.

Pour enough oil into a frying pan to half fill it and place on a high heat.

Once the oil is hot, use a large spoon to scoop the mixture from the mixing bowl into the frying pan and fry for 2–3 minutes, or until golden and crispy.

McKay's Carrot Cake

INGREDIENTS

A knob of butter for greasing
350 g plain flour
1 tsp baking powder
1 tsp bicarbonate of soda
A dash of salt
1 tsp ground cinnamon
1 tsp freshly grated nutmeg
4 medium eggs
350 g soft light brown sugar
1 tbsp vanilla extract
250 ml vegetable oil
400 g carrots
250 g raisins

METHOD

Preheat the oven to 160°/180° Fan/Gas 4. Grease a 34 cm x 24 cm baking tin and line with baking parchment.

In a bowl, combine the flour, baking powder, bicarbonate of soda, salt, cinnamon and nutmeg.

In a separate large bowl, whisk together the eggs, sugar, vanilla extract and vegetable oil using a hand-held mixer, for around five minutes until pale in colour.

Sift the dry ingredients into the wet ingredients and fold them in. Fold through the grated carrots and raisins until combined.

Pour the mixture into the prepared baking tin; it should be about half full so that the cake can rise without spilling over. Place in the centre of the oven and bake for 50 minutes to 1 hour until the cake is golden brown and springy to the touch.

Acknowledgements

The author would like to thank the following people for their work on this book.

Katie Levy – Editor
Joana Reis – Designer
Laura Pritchard – Senior Desk Editor
Naomi Greenwood – Copyeditor
Becca Allen – Proofreader
Joelyn Rolston-Esdelle – Production Manager
Dominic Kingston, Bec Gillies, Karis Pearson, Eleanor Bowskill – Marketing and Publicity
Berat Pekmezci – Cover Illustrator

'... **ENRICHING AND LIFE-AFFIRMING**'
INDEPENDENT

'... **POWERFUL WRITING BY AN AUTHOR WITH GREAT TALENT AND GREAT HEART**'
DAVID ALMOND

'**A MAJOR VOICE IN BRITISH CHILDREN'S LITERATURE**'
S. F. SAID

WELCOME TO CRONGTON, WHERE YOUR LOYALTY AND WITS WILL BE TESTED...

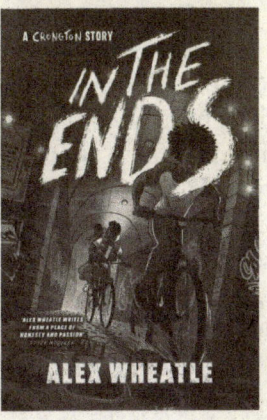

COLLECT ALL OF THE *CRONGTON* SERIES.

'GRIPPING'
MALORIE BLACKMAN

Alex Wheatle wrote several acclaimed novels, many of them inspired by experiences from his childhood. He was born in Brixton to Jamaican parents and spent most of his childhood in a Surrey children's home. After a short stint in prison following the Brixton uprising of 1981, he wrote poems and lyrics and became known as the Brixtonbard. Alex was shortlisted for numerous awards, including the Carnegie Medal and the YA Book Prize. He won the Guardian Children's Fiction Prize and was awarded an MBE for services to literature in 2008.

You can find out more about Alex here:

www.alexwheatle.com